The High-Skies Adventures of
BLUE JAY THE PIRATE

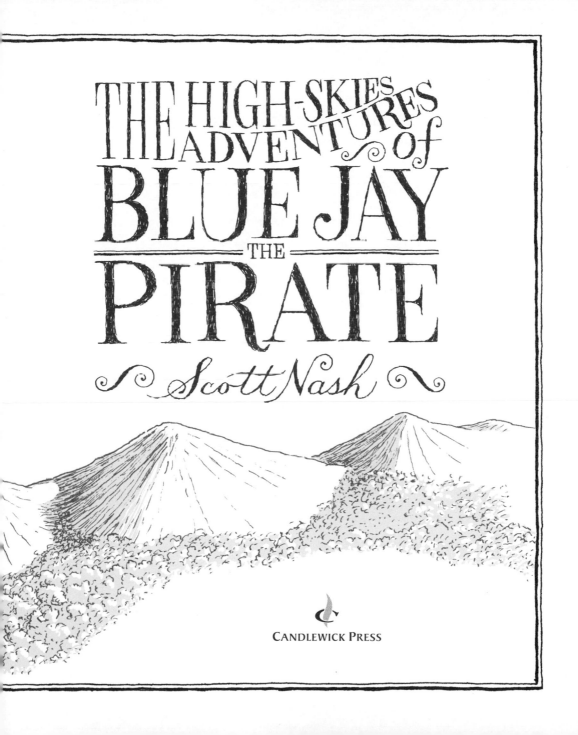

THE HIGH-SKIES ADVENTURES of BLUE JAY THE PIRATE

Scott Nash

CANDLEWICK PRESS

This book is gratefully dedicated to
Mary Lee Donovan, Ann Stott,
Scotty Whitehouse, and Nancy Gibson Nash.

Copyright © 2012 by Scott Nash

All rights reserved. No part of this book may be reproduced, transmitted, or
stored in an information retrieval system in any form or by any means,
graphic, electronic, or mechanical, including photocopying, taping, and
recording, without prior written permission from the publisher.

First edition 2012

Library of Congress Cataloging-in-Publication Data

Nash, Scott, date.
The high-skies adventures of Blue Jay the pirate / [text and illustration by Scott Nash]. — 1st ed.
p.   cm.
Summary: Blue Jay and his band of avian pirates sail the skies searching for ships
laden with cargo, avoiding run-ins with the dastardly crows, dodging doldrums and
bad weather, and evading the long arm of the Colonial army.
ISBN 978-0-7636-3264-9
[1. Birds — Fiction. 2. Pirates — Fiction. 3. Fantasy.]   I. Title.
PZ7.N17355Hi 2012
[E] — dc22   2010050563

12 13 14 15 16 17 SCP 10 9 8 7 6 5 4 3 2 1

Printed in Humen, Dongguan, China

This book was typeset in Bulmer.
The illustrations were done in tinted crow quill and ink.

Candlewick Press
99 Dover Street
Somerville, Massachusetts 02144

visit us at www.candlewick.com

A Riff on
Robert Louis Stevenson

∽

If flying ships to bird-sung tunes,
  Avian pirates, sparrows bold.
If weasels, fishers, and maroons
  And wicked crows their weapons sold,
And all the adventures, retold
  Exactly in the ancient way,
Can please you, as they pleased me in days of old,
  You wiser children of today:

So be it, and fall in! If not,
  If happy youth no longer crave,
Their daring fantasies forgot,
  Mowgli, or Jim Hawkins the brave,
Sherwood Forest prince and knave:
  So be it, also! And may I
And all my pirates share the grave
  Where these and their creations lie!

~ CONTENTS ~

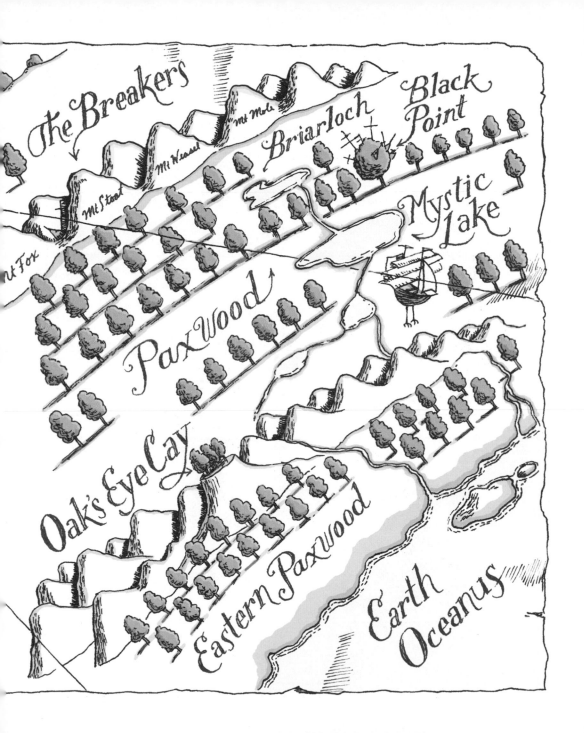

BLUE JAY

I

A RARE EGG, INDEED

Whilst fighting fearsome Finch's fleet,
    we've sung out, "Yo! Heave ho!"
And hearing hawks hanging high
    have I nobly faced the foe;
Then put round the grog, so we've
    that on our prog,
We'll laugh in strife's homely face,
    and sing, "Yo! Heave ho!"
We'll laugh in strife's homely face,
    and sing, "Yo! Heave ho!"

The captain of the *Grosbeak* had some strange and terrifying lore connected with his name. It was said, for instance, that Blue Jay would eat two or three songbird eggs for supper every evening. For this unspeakable horror, more than a few birds viewed him as a cannibal. Other reports held that he was immortal, an evil wizard, a shape-shifter, a scallywag, and generally the most bloodthirsty and fearsome pirate to sail the high skies. As a result, few ships' captains offered any resistance when they spotted Blue Jay's ship, the *Grosbeak*, flying the Jolly Robin, a black flag that bore the chilling image of a Thrush's skull laid over the crossed bones of the same.

Those who sailed with Blue Jay knew better and enjoyed a hearty laugh over the steady stream of stories regarding their commander's gruesome reputation. Yes, Blue Jay and his pirates could put on a spectacular show that would frighten the feathers off the crew of any ship they pursued. But, truth be told, the ghastly rumors amounted to a pack of lies. But this never bothered the pirate captain. Blue Jay understood the value of perpetuating useful lies, and he worked hard at keeping his reputation as loathsome and awful as possible.

As ruthless as he reportedly was, his crew knew him to be a stalwart optimist who was a fair, brave, merciful, and sometimes even wise captain. Mostly, he was a restless, intrepid adventurer whose enthusiasm infected the crew, and as a result, they would follow him to the ends of the earth to realize his audacious schemes and magnificent obsessions . . . Which brings us back to the subject of eggs.

The truth about Blue Jay and eggs was that he took great joy in stealing them, not as food but as treasure. He loved them as objects and had no interest at all in eating them. Hence, his egg collection was vast, filling an entire cabin with an extraordinary assortment of colors, shapes, and sizes. Occasionally, one of his collection would hatch, incubated accidentally in the warm hold of his ship. In fact, some of his crew had originated from eggs he collected:

Blackcap came from a subelliptical, creamy-white egg with fine, purplish-brown speckles; Thrasher from a long, greenish-blue egg with red-brown speckles; and Chuck-Will's-Widow from a large, elliptical, pinkish egg mottled with gray, purple, and brown.

"The trouble with eggs," Jay would often joke to his adopted offspring, "is that they sometimes grow legs!"

As convenient as it might seem to hatch your own crew, pirates like Jay are not the most dependable parents and are not well suited to having fluffy little chicks underfoot, tugging at the pirates' frocks and looking for someone to regurgitate food into their greedy, gaping mouths.

So, in recent years, Blue Jay had sworn off eggs in favor of other things that happened to fascinate him at any particular moment: jewels, contraptions of all sorts, weapons, and anything metal or shiny. As a result, his egg collection had had no new acquisitions for some time.

Then, one glorious spring morning, Blue Jay came to possess a new egg that was to change the fate and reputation of the pirates forever.

The pirates were digging up treasured acorns that they had buried during a previous journey along the shore of Long Pond. They were hauling a bundle from the sand when Junco, the ship's navigator, was nearly flattened by a very large egg that suddenly rolled out of the grass and onto the thin ice of the pond. It was chased by a half-crazed raccoon who had apparently stolen the egg from a nearby nest and was determined to have it for his lunch. The raccoon paused briefly at the icy shore and chattered angrily at the pirates, his back arched and fur spiking in every direction, making sure the crew understood that this was his egg and his alone. He snarled and bared his teeth as he loped and slipped across the icy surface, which promptly cracked, dunking the striped bandit into the frigid water below. This did not do much to slow the raccoon's progress as

he plowed determinedly through the brittle ice toward his lunch, which was spinning like a top on the surface of the pond.

The sight of that egg rekindled an old flame in Blue Jay's heart, and once again he was smitten. More than any that had come before, he just had to have that egg as part of his collection.

"Crayee!" he cried. "That's a rare egg, to be sure, and ours for the poaching!" He dispatched three of his crew — Junco, Thrasher, and Blackcap — to provide a distraction for the raccoon, and the pirates gleefully launched a relentless assault on the raccoon's head while Jay prepared to collect his prize from the pond.

"Lower Tarsus Six!" he called to the first mate, Crossbill.

"Lower Tarsus Six!" Crossbill echoed, and the order rang from the rigging, through the hold, and into the belly of the pirate ship floating in the air above them.

"Tarsus Six! Tarsus Six!" repeated the crew.

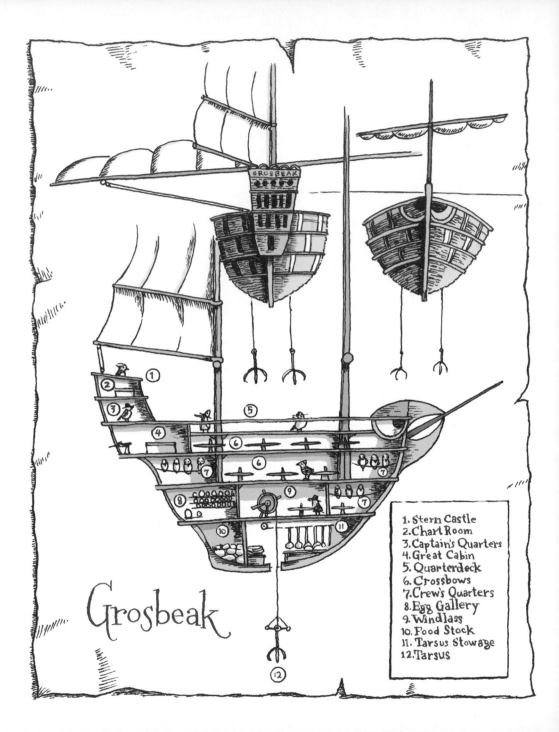

Grosbeak

1. Stern Castle
2. Chart Room
3. Captain's Quarters
4. Great Cabin
5. Quarterdeck
6. Crossbows
7. Crew's Quarters
8. Egg Gallery
9. Windlass
10. Food Stock
11. Tarsus Stowage
12. Tarsus

Tarsus is a word for a bird's leg. Jay's flying ship, the *Grosbeak,* had twelve tarsi altogether, or six pairs. Each of these was crafted out of hardwood and bits of metal, fashioned to perform a specific function. Some served as anchors; some were for cutting or bashing or drilling. Tarsus Six was used exclusively for grabbing.

So, Tarsus Six was lowered. Its large wooden claws shot open and then closed, ever so gently, around the shell. The egg was lifted from the ice, carried through the air, and set to rest on the deck of the *Grosbeak*. Once the egg was safely aboard, Junco, Thrasher, and Blackcap ceased their attack on the raccoon and promptly flew back to the ship. The poor, bewildered raccoon was left swimming in circles with nothing but the cold, sluggish fish and sleeping turtles in the frigid water deep below.

Chuck-Will's-Widow, a burly plug of a pirate with a particularly mean disposition, carried the weighty treasure down to the cabin in the belly of the ship, where Jay's egg collection was stored in a gallery. Chuck was a strong bird with sturdy legs, wide shoulders, and powerful wings, but his most prominent feature was his extraordinarily wide mouth, which extended from the tip of his sharp beak down to the top of his chest. Chuck was followed belowdecks by Junco, who, in contrast, was a modest ball of slate-gray feathers and was half the size of Chuck. She had a white chest, dark eyes, and a black cowl around her face that played up her pink beak. Junco was a brilliant navigator, a master sword fighter, and an earnest, scrappy sailor.

Chuck set the huge egg down carefully on a satin pillow, then stood back and frowned. Apart from its considerable size, the egg's appearance was unimpressive when compared with the colors and patterns of other eggs in collections past. "Rather homely mudder, says I!" Chuck stroked the bristles around his bill. "Hardly resembles a bird egg!"

Junco, who was inspecting the shell for cracks, was evidently annoyed by the comment. "Oh, it's a bird all right," she said in the egg's defense. "And prettier than the one you hatched out of, I'd wager." She then produced a soft cloth from the pocket of her waistcoat and began to polish the shell.

Chuck slapped the egg hard and laughed. He had a laugh that sounded like a wet cough. "Haw! No, ma'am! That's no bird egg! That there is a turtle! Likely a snapper, to boot! Haw!"

This ignited an argument between the two that went something like this:

"It's a bird!"

"Naw, I reckon it's a snake!"

"A bird!"

"Maybe a rattler! *Hisssssss!*"

"This is a bird egg, you idiot!"

And so on, until Blue Jay entered, whistling a familiar hauling song:

Roll! Roll! Roll in the egg, boys.
Roll in! Roll in! Away!

Pull! Pull! Pull the lines in.
Pull in! Pull in! Aweigh!

With a sweep of his wing, Jay motioned for Chuck and Junco to leave the cabin. Without a word, Chuck stepped out of the gallery, but Junco stayed behind, standing her ground with a certain, stubborn resolve.

"What's this?" said Jay. "Are you stuck to the floor there, Junco?"

Junco seemed flustered and blurted, "No, sir, I just thought you might want me to finish polishing the egg."

Jay inspected the egg. "You've done a fine job already," said Jay. "You can report on deck now. Make ready to sail. I need you at the helm, Junco."

But Junco remained.

Jay raised his brow disapprovingly, and after a brief stare-down, Junco turned and left the gallery and joined the crew to haul in the lines and set sail, away from the skies over Long Pond.

Alone in the gallery, Jay went back to inspecting the giant egg. He stroked its smooth surface with his wing feathers, rocked it from side to side, pecked at it a couple of times, and finally cawed loudly at it. Reasonably satisfied that the egg would not hatch, Blue Jay went back to the business of captaining a pirate ship, which entailed wandering all over the earth searching for big, fat ships to plunder.

2

MOBBING CALL

Billy! Wake up! Wake up, you fool!" came a voice from the darkness. The young sparrow startled, flapped his wings, and twitched his head every which way in an attempt to appear as if he was, and always had been, awake.

"Wasn't s-s-sleeping, Henry!" he slurred at his companion. "'Twas thinking, that's all. Thinking!"

"You were snoring!" said Henry, whose stern, stubby beak poked out of the hooded shawl that covered his head. "If Poppa Fox finds out that either of us has been sleeping on our watch, he'll have our flight feathers clipped and we'll be grounded for the season, slavin' in his kitchen for the rest of our lives, mark my word!"

The two sparrows were perched high in the tangle of vines that surrounded Briarloch, a poor farming village sitting near the banks of a nameless, thinly frozen pond in the middle of Paxwood Forest, which sprawled across the northern reaches of Thrushia. Briarloch was home to sixty or more sparrows, and as it was the middle of the night, most of them were sound asleep in their homes while a few stalwart sentries, including Billy and Henry, kept a watchful eye out for intruders. The two sparrows ruffled their feathers against the cold night. Though it was early spring, winter seemed determined to linger about and play cruel pranks on the season, dusting new blossoms with snow and glazing the soil with a crust of ice that foiled the farmers' attempts to till their fields.

The long winter had depleted much of the sparrows' stores, and food was dangerously scarce everywhere. These harsh conditions made for desperate times that turned

even decent, honest birds into thieves. Lately it seemed as if the forest — if not the entire colony — was swarming with all manner of thieves, bandits, migrants, and other ne'er-do-wells such as crows who thought nothing of plundering the stores of Thrushian villages. The Thrushian army was supposed to provide soldiers to protect their village. Lord knows they paid for it in the grain that they were forced to give the government after each harvest. Half of what they produced was shipped off to the capital every autumn, leaving the sparrows with barely enough food to make it through the winter. However, the residents of Briarloch had not seen a Thrushian soldier or official for five months, since the day their grain was shipped away. Since then, it seemed that the Thrushians were more interested in protecting their own stores rather than those of the poor farmers. With no assistance from the government, the sparrows had no choice but to defend themselves as best they could. The sparrows stored their grain in an area named the silo, a large, dome-shaped cave of briars that formed a nearly impenetrable shelter from wind and rain. It was so well protected that it was considered to be the safest area of the village, which was why younger, less experienced birds were chosen to sit watch there. It was considered a rite of passage, a step toward adulthood.

Henry and Billy were the best of friends and were especially pleased to be assigned to guard the silo together. They thought it would be good fun to stay up all night, eat breakfast before everyone else was awake, and then be able to sleep away most of the next day. Henry had warned Billy to get as much sleep as he could the day prior to their watch, but Billy paid him no mind and spent most of the afternoon practicing his sword and switching techniques. Now in the middle of the night, he was paying the price, and it wasn't long before he was once again dozing off to sleep.

"BILLY! YOU'RE SNORING AGAIN!"

"WAS NOT!" said Billy.

"You most certainly were!" said Henry.

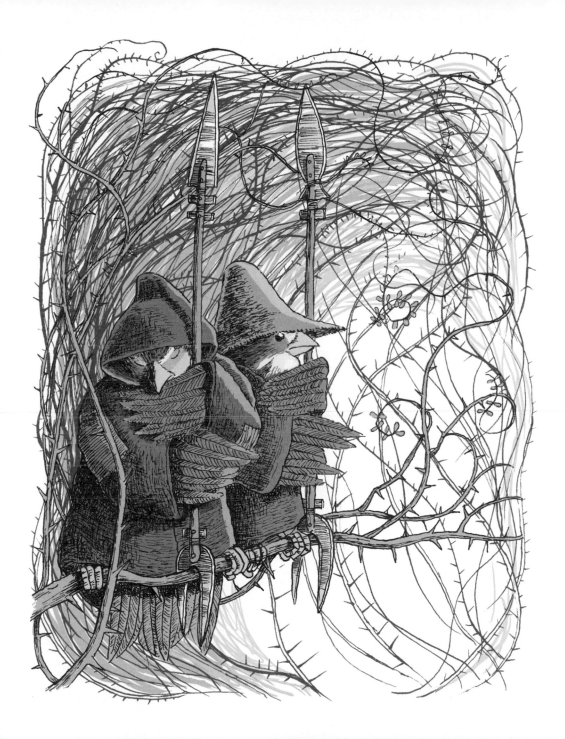

"I was pretending to snore," said Billy indignantly, "to fool them prowlers."

"Oh, yeah. Brilliant!" said Henry. "You'd fool them all right. You sounded like a snarling fisher cat. *Snorrk!*"

Billy joined in—"*Snorrrrrk!*"—and the two birds laughed till the cold squelched their humor.

"Crikes! It's cold!" cried Billy, ruffling his feathers. "I tell you, I almost wish a prowler would come along so I could warm myself by giving him a taste of my switch!"

"Why don't you practice, then? That'll warm you up enough," said Henry, fluffing up his feathers and pulling his hood tight. Switching was a form of self-defense involving a great deal of acrobatics with a staff or spear. The technique favored speed over strength and was very effective in fighting larger, slower creatures than themselves. Sparrows were required to learn how to use a switch soon after they were fledged, and it was common to see young sparrows practicing their technique for hours at a time.

On that night, Billy warmed himself by flying from branch to branch with his staff, spinning and lunging at invisible intruders, mostly crows. With each imaginary conquest, he shouted, "DIE, YE THIEVIN' PIRATE SCUM!" or "VICTORY!" or simply "ARRRGH!"

Henry laughed. "Quiet, Billy, or you'll wake up the entire village with your ranting!"

"At least they'll know we're awake and on guard!" said Billy "HA! DIE, HEATHEN!" He spun again and whacked at the briars a couple of times. Then, with a vicious thrust of his staff, he managed to get himself completely tangled in a dense knot of particularly thorny vines.

For a while Henry watched in amusement while Billy struggled to free himself from the brambles.

"Don't just sit there," Billy cried. "Help me, will ya?"

Henry flew to Billy and inspected the mess he was in. "You're really stuck here, mate."

"I know I'm stuck!" said Billy. "Please, just unhook me!"

21

"All right, then, but hold still! I can't get ahold of anything if you keep moving around."

Henry had just begun to pull away one of the thorns when from behind them they heard, "ARRAH, NOW!"

The two birds froze where they were.

"Oh, no!" Billy said under his breath.

"Is it him?" whispered Henry without turning to look.

On the ground below them stood a rotund, scowling sparrow named Poppa Fox and two other large, thuggish-looking characters named Covey and Cyrus. Though they were the same age, Henry and Billy did not get along with Covey and Cyrus, who apparently enjoyed nothing more than relentlessly harassing smaller birds as a way to show off their superior size and strength. They smirked cruelly at Henry and Billy's predicament.

Poppa Fox leaned on his switch and squinted into the brambles. "WHAT IN THE HECK 'N' HELL IS GOIN' ON IN HERE?" he growled.

Poppa Fox was the owner of the Sooty Fox inn and tavern and was, without argument, the most respected of the village elders. A veteran of the Colonial War, he had lost his left leg in battle and relied on a peg leg fashioned out of a twig to hop from place to place. Poppa Fox had a personality that matched his substantial girth. He could be exceedingly kind when pleased and furious as a hurricane when riled. Poppa Fox was clearly in one of his stormier moods that night. "WOLL?" he bellowed. "I'M WAITING!"

Billy stammered, "W-well, P-P-P-Poppa, I was p-practicing with my switch, you see . . . I was . . ." Billy's courage left him, and his voice trailed off behind it.

Henry chimed in for his friend. "Sorry, Poppa. We were trying to stay warm by practicing our switching."

Poppa Fox's face darkened a bit more. "Yor not here to play games. Yor here to be on the lookout for intruders. Nothing is growing these days, and our rations are low. There's no tellin' how long this stinkin' cold's gonna last, and we can't afford to have what's left of our food stolen!"

"Yes, Poppa!" said Henry and Billy together.

"Covey! Cyrus!" Poppa Fox barked. "Don't just stand there smirking! Help Henry get Billy out of there, will you?"

The brutes flew to Billy and set to their task eagerly, shoving Henry out of the way and yanking Billy out of the briars, tearing his clothes in the process. Before releasing Billy, Covey pulled him close and hissed in his ear, "You woke me from me sleep, doofus! There'll be hell ta pay later, mark my words!"

Again wings rattled in the cold night. They did not sound like sparrow wings, and a sudden chill ran down Henry's spine. "W-what are they?" he whispered.

"I'll bet I know who it is!" growled Billy. Then he hollered, "COVEY! CYRUS! WE KNOW YOU'RE DOWN THERE! MOVE ON OUT OF HERE, OR WE'LL COME FLUSH YOU OUT!"

There was no answer, but the briars on which they were perched vibrated a bit. Henry had a particularly keen sense of vibration, and while he wasn't able to identify the source, he was certain that the vibrations were not coming from sparrows but from something else. They were too pronounced, too big, too powerful. Much too big to be either Covey or Cyrus. But before he could say anything, Billy shouted, "SHOW YERSELVES, YE COWARDS!"

"Shhh!" warned Henry. "I have a bad feeling here. . . ."

"I've had it with these blokes," cried Billy, who grabbed his switch and spun in the air. "Let's go get 'em, Henry!"

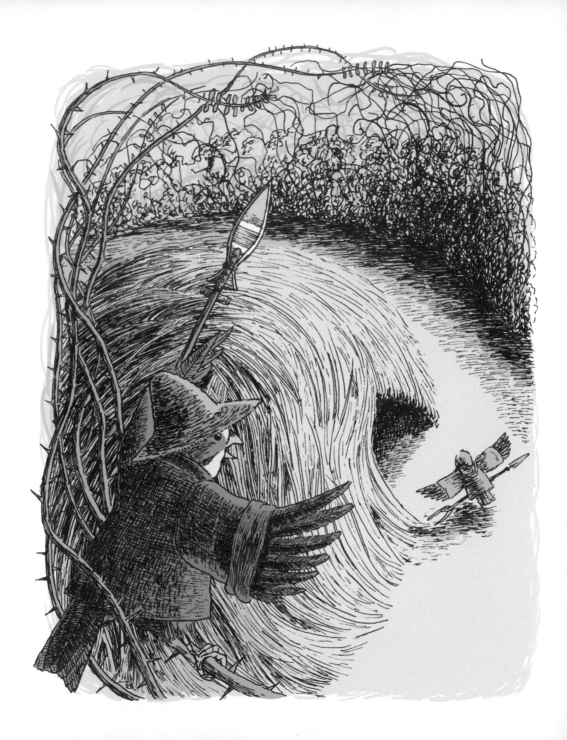

"Wait! Billy, don't!" said Henry, but it was too late. Billy dove toward the silo and was out of sight. Henry hesitated for only a moment, then reached for his switch and followed his friend.

There was a more distant sound of flapping in the darkness followed by a sickening silence. Henry slowed his flight as he approached the silo. Billy was nowhere to be seen.

"Billy?" he called softly. A dreadful chill coursed through his heart. "Billy?" he tried again. Henry perched himself on one of the vines that lined the silo walls. He sat very still, even though inside he was spinning like a gyroscope. He scanned the area — still no sign of Billy. His attention focused on the ground around the silo. It was covered with footprints that were easily four times the size of any sparrow's.

"Crows!" Henry said under his breath. Panic swept through him, and he shouted the alarm: "CROWS IN THE SILO! CROWS IN THE SILO!"

At that, a mob of black birds erupted from the silo entrance. Henry swung his switch at one of them, but the force of the larger bird threw him to the ground and his face slammed into the dirt. He felt a sharp pain in his head and chest and could barely recover his breath. With great effort, he turned over and found himself facing a great hulking crow, dressed entirely in black except for a tall, pointed, black-and-gray-striped hat. His black beak was highly polished and bore a sharp, cruel smile. He held a sack of seed in one wing and a bludgeon in the other. Henry recognized him; Bellamy was part of a notorious gang of crows that plagued Briarloch and seemed to despise little brown birds more than anything. This mob, led by the infamous Teach, would go out of its way to harass sparrows whenever the opportunity presented itself.

"Dirty, filthy sparra!" spat Bellamy, Teach's brother, raising his club. "HA!" He laughed as he knocked Henry senseless with a blow to the side of the head. Henry crumpled in the dirt, and the world went black as a crow.

BELLAMY

◌◌◌◌

Two days later, Henry awoke to find himself lying in a healing nest, his head held steady in Poppa Fox's wings. He moved slightly and groaned as his head thumped and rattled with pain.

"There now, lie still, me boy," Poppa Fox said soothingly. "Don't move. Ye need to rest. Ye took quite a punch. Cracked yor nut badly, I'm afraid."

Henry glanced up to see the innkeeper's tired, kind face and tried to sort out what was happening. In the opaque predawn light, he could make out the shadowy figures of other sparrows, their movements slow and sorrowful. Beyond them Henry noticed an oblong basket draped with a black shroud. "Billy?" he said, pulling away from the old bird and sitting suddenly upright, remembering. But the pressure and pain in his head pulled him back down. "Where's Billy?" he cried, half knowing the terrible answer.

Poppa Fox lowered his head and shook it slowly from side to side.

Henry persisted. "Billy! Where is he?"

Poppa Fox said nothing, but Henry could see the answer in the old bird's eyes. It was Billy in that black-shrouded basket.

"BILLY!" he sobbed as he struggled to get up but fell, unconscious once more, into the wings of Poppa Fox.

3

JUNCO'S VIGIL

Blast! Where is that bird?" shouted the *Grosbeak*'s quartermaster. Snipe was a taciturn, hard-bitten shorebird with a
stocky build, strong legs, large claws, and a beak as long
and as sharp as a cutlass. He was more dapper than most
quartermasters, wearing a striped coat with fine piping
and metal buttons. He was never without a sash around
his waist, a scarf about his neck, and spectacles perched
upon his beak. To give himself an added air of authority,
he topped his outfit with a stovepipe hat, which made him
appear taller than the other birds. As with his own dress,
Snipe held the crew to high standards in their work and
behavior and watched them with a relentless, critical eye.

SNIPE

It was Snipe's responsibility to make certain that each sailor did his or her fair share of the work and to dole out discipline to any who shirked his or her duties. So when Junco failed to appear for her watch the morning after the mysterious egg was brought on board, Snipe called on Creeper, a good friend of Junco's, to go seek her out. "Creeper!" yelled Snipe. "Search this ship stem to stern! I want Junco on deck in three turns of a ship's wheel!"

"Aye, sir!" Creeper hurried down the hatch.

Creeper did not take long. After a cursory search of the sleeping berths and a peek into the hold, he pointed his curved beak toward the Egg Gallery, where he found Junco sitting, of all places, on top of the stolen egg, fast asleep. Creeper chuckled at the sight, but Junco did not stir.

Feeling mischievous and as a bit of a joke, Creeper sidled up close to his friend, put his beak right up to her ear, and in a loud whisper said, "Psssst! Hey, matey, wake up!" Creeper was not prepared for Junco's reaction to this.

Instead of simply startling awake, Junco let out an ear-piercing screech, spun around, and pinned poor Creeper to the floor, where he soon found himself with a sword and dirk pointed directly at his chest.

Creeper was terrified. "S-s-spare me, friend!" he wailed. "I come on Mr. S-S-Snipe's orders. Ya missed yer watch!"

Junco relaxed, recognizing her friend. "Sorry, old boy, but you gave me a start!" she said, putting away her weapons. "You caught me in the middle of a nightmare—a gang of raccoons was trying to steal our treasure here." She patted the egg.

"Thasss all right, Junco," said Creeper as he brushed himself off. "No harm done. . . . I shouldn't've s-s-sneaked up on ya."

"I'm just glad I didn't hurt my old friend," said Junco, patting him on the shoulder. "Now, let's get back to work, shall we?"

"Yesss!" said Creeper, relieved. "Mr. Snipe is waiting—" Junco then surprised him as she flew in the air and settled herself right back down on the egg.

"Junco, my friend," Creeper cautioned meekly, "you can't s-s-stay here. S-S-Snipe's in a s-s-snit already on account of you missing your watch."

Junco's expression darkened. "I can't leave this egg, Creeper. I can't. The poor thing is cold!"

Creeper shifted uncomfortably. "What sh-sh-should I tell S-S-Snipe?"

Junco thought for a moment. "Please tell Snipe that I'm indisposed."

"Beg your pardon?" said Creeper.

"Tell him that I'm sick," said Junco.

He tried to appeal to his friend, but finally, when it was clear that Junco would not budge, Creeper had to deliver the bad news to Snipe.

"What do you mean she's sitting on the egg!" the quartermaster clacked. "Does she plan to hatch the thing? I won't stand for it, I tell you!" Snipe began to march off with long strides. "I'll remove Junco from that egg myself!"

"But, s-s-sir!" Creeper cried after him.

Snipe wheeled around. "Yes, Mr. Creeper?" he snapped. "What is it now?"

"S-s-s-sir, b-b-beggin' your p-pardon, b-but sh-sh-sh-she's armed, s-s-sir!"

Snipe contemplated this for a moment, had a change of heart, and decided instead to order the two largest birds on the ship to "convey" Junco to the poop deck. Thrasher and Chuck-Will's-Widow stood before Snipe, who held a generous coil of rope. "Tie her up if you must," said the quartermaster. "I want that rascal on deck immediately!" And he tossed the rope to Chuck.

"I won't need this," said Chuck with a sneer as he handed the rope to Thrasher. "It's only Junco." And with that, the two hulking birds went below to fetch their shipmate.

Blue Jay was in his cabin with Crossbill, poring over charts and maps, planning what Jay referred to as "Ship fishin'" or "Fishin' for ships."

"I can see it in me head," he said. "A big ship under full sail in a stiff westerly wind, barely moving, so fat 'n' heavy is she with stores and treasure! Hoo! Hoo! Crossbill, we have a profitable adventure ahead of us, I reckon! With any luck, we'll soon have an abundance of seed and shiny objects in our possession!"

40

"Shiny objects that we will, no doubt, proceed to bury underground," said Crossbill with a bit of a smirk.

"Of course we will!" said Jay, focusing his attention once again on the pile of charts in front of him.

"Why do we do that?" asked Crossbill.

"Do what?" said Blue Jay as he gazed at the map with the help of a small cylindrical looking glass.

"Why do we bury treasure?"

Jay looked up and laughed. "We're pirates! It's what we do!" He unrolled one of the maps. "Besides, we can't bring it all with us. . . . I mean, just look at all of the locations in which we have buried booty!" Jay hopped to a rope that hung across the table directly above the map and began pecking at points where the pirates had buried treasure. "Here and here and here and, let's see . . . here." He pecked until the map was covered with divots made by the tip of his bill. He sat back with a satisfied smile. "It would take an armada of the largest colonial ships imaginable to carry that amount of booty!" he bragged.

"Perhaps more, for you have forgotten Bowline Notch!" said Crossbill, tapping the map with a stick.

"Really?" said Blue Jay, peering forward.

"And Red Crest."

Tap!

"And Spar Cove."

Tap!

"You're joking!" said Blue Jay, taking a closer look.

"Oh, and Fog Hollow, Thunder Hole, and Long Pond."

Tap! Tap! Tap!

Crossbill smiled crookedly and traced the map with the point of his stick. "That's six you have forgotten. Let's see if there are more. . . ."

They were interrupted by a sudden commotion from belowdecks. They heard muffled cries, crashes, and cracks that made the hull shudder.

"Cryee!" said Jay. "It sounds as if we're under attack from the inside out!" They flew immediately out of the cabin and to the rail above, where Snipe was standing.

"Status, Mr. Snipe!" said Jay as the tremors and shouts continued. "What is that racket?"

"I'm afraid Junco's gone mad, sir!" said Snipe. "She's with that egg!"

Before Jay could issue an order, the commotion ceased, and Thrasher and Chuck reappeared on deck, looking stunned and disheveled. Thrasher carried Junco's hat, sword, and dirk, but the navigator herself was nowhere to be seen.

Snipe frowned. "Well, where is she, then?"

Chuck stood with his mouth clamped shut and his crop grossly distended.

Thrasher cleared his throat. "Well, Junco, ya see . . . she put up quite a fight. . . ." he began.

"Yes, and?" said Snipe impatiently.

"We had to take drastic measures," said Thrasher.

"Yes, well, get on with it!" said Snipe. "Where is Junco?"

Thrasher continued, "Chuck here has, ah, swallowed her, sir."

Chuck's crop bulged even more, and his head jerked violently from side to side.

"Swallowed her! Chuck!" said Snipe. "Drop her! Do you hear me, Chuck? Drop Junco at once!"

Chuck seemed only too glad to comply. He leaned toward the deck and opened his large mouth just a crack. Junco came bursting out, angry as a boil and itching for a fight. She flew directly at Chuck and sent him reeling with

CHUCK-WILL'S-WIDOW

a series of sharp pecks between the eyes. Next she wrestled her hat from Thrasher and pulled it onto her head, seized her sword and dirk, then stood, damp and defiant on deck, ready to fight off anyone who came near her.

Snipe wasn't having it. In one swift motion, he snatched Junco up by her collar while Chuck and Thrasher seized her by the wings. The sword and the dirk fell to the deck, and Snipe snapped his long beak at her. "I'll have no more of this nonsense, do you hear me!" he said. "Settle down or I'll have that blasted egg thrown overboard immediately!" Snipe glanced up toward Blue Jay. "With the captain's permission, that is."

Jay gestured for Snipe to continue.

Junco struggled for a moment, then quieted, hanging suspended between her shipmates. "You missed yer watch, sailor," said Snipe. "And that won't stand, not on my ship! I'm havin' you lashed to the wheel, where you will stand three watches: one for yer missed watch, one for brawling with the crew, and one for insubordination!"

Snipe leaned in close to Junco. "And if I hear so much as a peep out of you, why, I'll give you three watches tomorrow as well!"

Jay nodded, and so it was that Junco and the egg were separated. Junco was hauled away to begin the first of what would be nine miserable hours at the wheel.

Jay turned to Crossbill. "Now that's a shame!" he said with a sigh. "What do you suppose has gotten into Junco, eh, Bill? She's a good bird generally, don't you think?"

"I can't say what happened for sure, Captain, though it's true that Junco missed her watch, so it is right that she be called out for it." Crossbill then added, "Snipe is a fair quartermaster. Fair, and tough as nails."

Jay stroked his chin and shook his head. "I suppose you are right, but still . . ." Then Jay shrugged off the thoughts that were troubling him and said, "Let's get back to our charts, shall we, and leave Snipe to manage the affairs of the crew."

With that, the two returned to their charts.

Try as he might, however, Jay could not get his mind off his navigator's strange behavior. Soon enough, he excused himself and made his way to the helm and Junco.

Junco was steering a straight-enough course from her tether, but she was staring, glassy-eyed, and mumbling, as though deranged. "Leave me be," she kept repeating. "Just leave me be."

Jay came up alongside her. "Ten degrees to port, Junco!" he said. "Bear toward that cargo ship ahead."

This seemed to snap Junco out of her trance. "Yes, Captain!" she said, standing up straight, gripping the wheel with authority, and turning the ship ten degrees to the left. She squinted anxiously into the distance to catch a glimpse of the ship that she had evidently missed.

"She's a fat one, isn't she, Junco?" Blue Jay said. "Filled to the eyes with treasure, but, judging by the way she's sitting low in the air, I'll also wager she's armed to the teeth. Wouldn't you agree?"

Junco leaned forward, straining to see this vessel.

Finally, she had to confess, "Sir, your eyes must be far superior to mine, for I can't see a thing ahead."

"That's a shame. She's a beauty, all right. Too bad she's still three or four days away from here."

Junco looked warily at the captain and then said flatly, "That's remarkable, sir. You can see three days' distance. That would be, let's see . . . six hundred miles. Very good, sir!"

Blue Jay laughed. "Crayee, Junco, no! I'm not using me eyes!" He pointed to his forehead. "I see the ship in me mind, not every detail, but I see enough." Junco looked understandably skeptical, and Jay continued, "Remember that ship we took last week? What was it called?"

Junco thought for a moment. "It was the *Murrelet*."

"Well, I tell you, I saw the *Murrelet* two days before our encounter." Jay tapped his forehead. "'Twas in here that I knew she was carrying a load of seed. And I was right, by thunder! And where is that seed now? Why, it's in our hold, isn't it?"

Junco gave no answer, and Jay paused, perhaps to study the clouds or the invisible ship ahead, before saying, "I'll tell you true. I'm good with the ships, but there is much my mind can't imagine." Jay bent back the brim of Junco's hat and looked her in the eye. "For instance, I can't see what you see in that egg below. Tell me, Junco: what are ya seein' in that egg, in yer mind's eye?"

Junco was at a loss. The truth was she could not see anything in that egg, at least not in the way that Jay was describing. She was one of the most skilled navigators of the high skies. She could discern, in advance, where the favorable prevailing winds would be or where the windless doldrums lay. She could read the sky: the patterns of the clouds, the movements of the sails, and birds soaring all had meaning to her. There were many times that she had directed the *Grosbeak* out of danger and into fortune's path by seeing and sensing things that others could not. Nevertheless, she was unfamiliar with the "mind pictures" that Jay spoke of. She couldn't "see" what was in the egg any more clearly than she could see Jay's merchant ship on the horizon.

"It's more of a feel," Junco said half to herself, but Jay caught it and responded immediately.

"Eh?" he said. "What is this 'feel' you're talkin' about? Come on, tell me now. If you can describe it, perhaps I can picture it."

Junco mulled the question for a while. "Adventure," she said. "I feel there is adventure in that egg."

Jay perked up. "Go on!" he said. "What sort of adventure?"

Emboldened, Junco said, "A rare thing, sir. A creature we've never known before. One of the ancients, perhaps . . . maybe a raven or a firebird or even a thunderbird."

Jay scratched his chin thoughtfully. "A thunderbird, you say? Having a bird like that on our side could be advantageous."

Thunderbirds were large mythic birds described as capable of conjuring powerful winds, stormy skies, and thunderous claps of thunder with every beat of their powerful wings. Every time a thunderbird blinked, it was said, lightning flashed.

"You do think it's alive?" Jay pressed.

"Oh, sir, I am certain of it!" said Junco. "There's something powerful in that egg!"

Jay closed his eyes. "Wait, wait . . . I'm seeing something. . . ." He seemed to be in a trance. "It's blobby, fuzzy. . . . It's a bird! . . . I think." Junco waited with anticipation. Then, suddenly, Jay opened his eyes wide. Junco held her breath. "I still can't see the thing," he said, shaking his head. "Tell you what, though. I'll meditate on it for a spell." Jay began to walk away.

"Wait! Please, Captain!" called Junco. "There isn't time! That egg needs to be kept warm or whatever's inside will die! I beg you, release me from this watch and let me hatch the poor thing."

Junco's plea was loud enough to attract the attention of some of the crew, including Snipe. "Is there a problem, Captain?" he called.

"No, not at all," Jay replied. He turned back to Junco. "Mr. Snipe is me quartermaster, and I stand by his judgment," he said, then more quietly he added, "But keep yer spirits up, Junco. Steer us a steady course, and I'll take care of the egg."

It would suffice to say that the crew of the *Grosbeak* did not take kindly to the orders they received from their captain that afternoon. Jay required that each pirate be given a two-hour stint during which he or she must sit upon the mysterious egg to keep it warm.

"I didn't become a sailor to hatch no stinkin' egg!" griped Chuck-Will's-Widow.

" 'S not natural!" growled an indignant Thrasher.

"That egg drove poor ol' Junco off her nut!" said Chuck.

"It's bad fortune, I tell you," said Blackcap. "An evil ovum!"

Unfortunately, no one understood his joke.

STRANGE HATCHLING

It was a whisker after midnight the following night when the crew of the *Grosbeak* was startled awake by loud, bellowing cries coming from the Egg Gallery.

"MURDER! I'M SLAIN!" Then again, "MURDER!" followed by a long, croaking moan that raised the birds' head feathers. "OOOOHHHHH! OOOOWWW!"

"That's Chuck!" said Thrasher, bounding off his perch. "He's with that cursed egg!"

The whole crew sprang into action, armed themselves, and raced to the gallery. There they found Chuck rolling on the floor, holding his tail end, and crying out in pain. "OOOOHHHHHHHHHOOOOOWWWW!"

"Chuck, wot's happened?" asked Thrasher.

"The devil attacked me in me sleep." He groaned again. "OOOOHHHHHHOOOOOWWWW!"

The moonlight spilling through an open hatch revealed scattered pieces of broken shell on the gallery floor.

On seeing this, most of the pirates stepped back, but brave Blackcap flew to his friend's side while keeping one eye and the point of his sword fixed on a dark corner. "Where is the thing?" demanded Blackcap.

"The monster bit me rump!" cried Chuck.

"Yes, but where is it?" cried Blackcap.

"Tore out me tail feathers, it did!" wailed Chuck.

"Blast it! Tell me where the monster is!" yelled Blackcap.

The big bird groaned and said, "It's behind them baskets over in the corner!"

Something slid in the darkness followed by the sound of a crash and a sharp *"Hissss! Hissss! Hissss!"*

"SNAAAAKE!" cried the pirates. In complete terror, they scrabbled and scratched and clawed their way back up the ladder and onto the main deck.

Chuck brought up the rear, holding his own and adding to the panic by hollering, "MOVE! MOVE! IT'S RIGHT BEHIND ME!" The pirates clambered on deck, slammed the hatches shut, and bolted them tight.

"WHAT'S GOING ON HERE?" called Snipe, buttoning his shirt and adjusting his hat as he appeared at his cabin door.

The crew was in an uproar, all talking at once about

the monstrous black serpent that was apparently slithering just under their feet.

Jay appeared at the rail and signaled to Snipe to calm the panicky pirates.

"SILENCE!" ordered Snipe. "Y'ALL SOUND LIKE A BUNCH OF GUINEA HENS! SILENCE, I SAY!"

The crew quieted, and Jay spoke. "Somebody tell me what is going on here."

This set the crew to speaking at once. "A SERPENT! THE DEVIL HISSELF! A SNAKE! A MONSTER!"

"SCREEEE! SCREEEEEEEEEEE!" Jay screamed in a perfect imitation of a red-tailed hawk. It was so convincing that the entire crew, including Snipe, hit the deck and fell into a cowering silence. "Now, one at a time," said Jay. "Let's start with a sensible voice, such as, let's see . . . Junco, tell us what has happened, will ye?" Jay scanned the crew, and the crew turned their heads around. Jay felt a sudden surge of panic. "WHERE IS JUNCO?" demanded the captain.

Junco was sound asleep belowdecks. Exhausted by three consecutive watches and satisfied that her precious egg was safe, Junco had fallen into a very deep slumber in a quiet corner of the sleeping berth toward the bow of the ship. She had not heard any of the commotion in the gallery, nor had she woken when the hatches were slammed shut. It was brave little Creeper who slipped below to find her. He had promised to let Junco know as soon as the egg began to hatch, so there he was, standing in front of her, not knowing what to do. He was terrified by the serpent but perhaps more terrified by once again startling his friend awake. "Jun-co!" he whispered as he gently shook her. "Junco, wake up!"

"Wha? What's happening?" Junco said groggily. Then her eyes widened at the site of Creeper. "Is it? Has it—?"

"It'sss hatched," confirmed Creeper.

The news sent Junco into a flurry, and Creeper shied away. Junco bounced around the cabin, grabbed food from baskets, stuffed her pockets, and exclaimed, "I hope someone's fed the poor thing!" and "We need to keep it warm!" and "The first few moments of a chick's life are very important!"

Creeper tried to speak, but between Junco's excitement and his stutter, he could not get a word in edgewise.

"Here! Take this," said Junco, depositing a basket of green leaves into Creeper's wings. "Bring this along, will you, please?" And with that, Junco flew out of the cabin toward the Egg Gallery at the far end of the ship.

"Junco!" Creeper cried, flying after her. "Wait! S-s-s-stop! It'sss not a chick!"

But Junco was already gone. Creeper followed, feeling sick, and peered cautiously into the darkness of the Egg Gallery. There he was relieved to find Junco alive but shocked to see her offering a few leaves of watercress to the creature that was still hidden in the darkness. Junco was speaking in a thin, hushed voice. "There, there, little one. Nothing to fear now. Mama's here."

Mama? thought Creeper. *She has gone mad.* Junco

confirmed his fear by actually putting a sprig of watercress in her beak and presenting it to the creature. Creeper couldn't believe the situation they were in: he and Junco (who was apparently stark-raving mad) alone with some sort of monster lurking in the darkness. He simply could not stand it anymore and shouted, "JUNCO! C-COME AWAY FROM THERE! IT'S D-D-D-DANGEROUS!" Sure enough, something hissed again, very close to where Junco was perched.

Junco took the leaves out of her mouth and turned to Creeper. "Stop your shouting," she whispered. "You're scaring the wits out of him."

"Scaring the wits out of *him*?" Creeper answered. "That s-s-snake th-thing tried to eat Chuck."

Junco laughed softly. "It's no snake, Creeper. Come see for yourself." And with that, she placed the cress back in her bill and offered it to the darkness.

Creeper nearly fainted when a shiny black mouth darted

out and grabbed the food from Junco. The mouth was connected not to a snake but to a fluffy black-and-yellow head,
which followed Junco's every movement, its eyes searching
for more watercress.

It was then that the hatch above their heads swung
open, and Jay flew into the gallery with his sword drawn.
"Stand back, both of you! I'll deal with . . . save you
from . . ." He paused. "Cryeeee! What have we hatched
there?!"

"It's a gosling!" answered Junco happily.

"A gosling? Well, I'll be!" said Jay with a broad smile.
"Hmmm. Almost as good as a thunderbird, I'd say!"

The rest of the crew peered down cautiously from the
hatch above, keeping a safe distance while trying to catch a
glimpse of the strange new passenger. When they did, they
couldn't help uttering a collective *"Awwwwwww!"*

The baby goose was a gangly little creature covered
in yellow down. He had large black webbed feet, a shiny

black beak, and dark eyes that gave him a determined sort of cuteness. His wings flapped uselessly as he lunged for the watercress Junco held out to him.

"He's a hungry little devil," Jay said with a laugh. "Take care he doesn't take yer wing tips along with those leaves."

"Aye, he's going to need more food soon. And water," said Junco.

"'Tis bad luck to bring water on board a ship," came the stern voice of Snipe, who was standing shoulder to shoulder with Crossbill in the doorway. But when the quartermaster saw the little goose gobble up the remaining greens and look adoringly at Junco, he softened a bit, adjusted his glasses, and said, "Well, let me have a look at this tot here."

The gosling teetered to its full height, nearly eye to eye with Snipe, and started hissing and spitting again and flapping its tiny wings. Snipe stepped back and removed his glasses. Wiping the lenses with a handkerchief, he sighed, clicked his bill a few times, then said, "As you are no doubt aware, Captain, what we have standing before us is a *Branta* goose, otherwise known as a black goose. Many believe geese and their like to be descended from gods. Whether or not you believe that sort of foolishness, having a gosling on board is a dangerous proposition. An adult black goose is one of the meanest creatures in the world. Without provocation, it will attack anyone who crosses its path. Just think what one of them would do to someone who's kidnapped one of its own. A full-grown *Branta* is about the size of our ship. Its long, powerful wings could easily snap our masts in two." Snipe paused, then smiled sarcastically. "All that aside, I congratulate you on your latest . . . treasure."

Blue Jay whistled in amazement. "Well, thank you, Snipe. That was certainly informative," he said. "While we decide what to do about this young, ah, *Branta,* do you, um . . . have any ideas for how we might care for this little 'godling' in the meantime?"

"Care for him?" said Snipe, startled. "You must be joking, sir! We can't keep this —"

"Yes, we can — we must!" interrupted Junco. "He thinks we're his parents!"

"Silence!" Snipe hissed. "This conversation is between the captain and myself. One more outburst from you, Junco, and I swear I'll have you locked up in the hold."

Wisely, Junco chose to shut her beak.

"All right, then, Snipe," said Jay. "What do you suggest we do?"

"On your orders, sir," Snipe began, with a cautioning glance at Junco, "I would recommend that we leave the gosling on the shore of the nearest pond straightaway, before his presence on our ship is discovered and a much, much bigger goose — er, problem — descends upon us."

Junco's eyes blazed and her feathers fluffed. Protective feelings for the gosling burned in her chest, yet she kept her beak shut.

Junco's agitation did not go unnoticed. In fact, many of the pirates shared her sadness and disappointment over Snipe's practical but harsh recommendation.

The crew stood, shuffling their feet nervously, staring at the floor awkwardly and holding their breath, waiting for his decision while a gosling who was taller than most of them just kept on peeping loudly and insistently for more food. Standing stiffly by her mates was Junco, puffed up and stormy, looking like a little gray dandelion about to explode with the slightest hint of a breeze.

Jay issued no order. Instead, he was the one who

exploded . . . in laughter. "HA! HA! HA-HA-HA-HA!" Both the gosling and the crew were stunned into silence by his outburst. They stared at him, dumbstruck, as Jay laughed and laughed. When he finally stopped, he wiped tears from his eyes. "HOOOO-WEE," he said. "I say this . . . we will let the gosling be our guest for a day or two or three. We'll keep him out of sight, and then we'll figure out how to go about finding him a proper home."

Snipe stood tall and sharply inhaled his disapproval while the crew exhaled their relief. The pirates peered down affectionately at the gosling, who smiled up at them for the first time. Blackcap, who was a bit of a wise guy, teased, "Will ye look at that? Ain't that the sweetest little chick Chuck's hatched there?"

Chuck frowned and croaked, "As I recollect, Chickadee, we *all* hatched this egg."

"Indeed, we did," said Blackcap, "but surely ye see how much the baby resembles you! Just look at the size of that mouth, fer instance!"

For the moment, the pirates were smitten by the young *Branta*. Someone suggested that the gosling needed a name. They joked with names like Slither, Hisster, and Yellow Snake. Finally, Chuck-Will's-Widow said simply, "Gabriel . . . his name is Gabriel." When asked why, he said, "I dunno. It's just his name." And that it was.

Two days passed, then two weeks, then two months, and Gabriel remained on the *Grosbeak*. As spring warmed into summer, food became more plentiful and Gabriel grew to an astonishing size. While he was the youngest on board, he was already the largest, yet he was still in downy feathers and unable to fly. He had outgrown two sets of clothing, and Junco was obliged to start adding panels of spare cloth whenever and wherever they were needed. Gabriel's jacket was growing into a patchwork of the crew's cast-offs, the remnants of clothing, tattered flags, and old pieces of sailcloth.

The pirates had become Gabriel's teachers, and the

GABRIEL

Grosbeak was his schoolhouse. The goose turned out to be a quick study and could soon name nearly all of the sails and lines. His favorites were the wing sails, the long mainsails that reached out toward the horizon. He would stare at the sails and stretch out his short wings, willing them to grow so that he, too, could fly.

The goose proved to be a cheerful and helpful member of the crew. Or at the very least, he tried his best to be. He had a strong neck and back, which were useful for lifting and hauling sacks and gear, a task that he willingly performed throughout the day. In most other ways, however, the poor goose was ridiculously ill suited to life on board a ship. His ability to move around the decks comfortably was hampered by his large webbed feet, which were designed for flat, solid ground and not for perching or grabbing onto ropes and rigging.

Since none of the pirates had any useful knowledge or experience raising a goose, let alone a godling, they simply decided to raise him as a pirate. Junco spent hours training the goose in all aspects of pirate life, including fighting with a sword and a switch. Gabriel's first attempt to use a switch proved to be a mistake, as switches require agility and the ability to spin tightly in the air. Junco had a bit more success training the goose to use a sword. What Gabriel lacked in skill, he made up for in strength and enthusiasm. Unfortunately, having a huge, clumsy, eager gosling running around deck wielding a sharp blade did not always go over well with the rest of the crew.

Jay, on the other hand, was never anything but delighted with Gabriel's progress. "Cripes, Snipe!" he said one warm, cloudless day while he, Crossbill, and Snipe were watching a sparring session. "That *Branta* is as strong as five birds."

"Indeed, he is, sir," Snipe grumbled. "He also eats enough for *ten* birds!"

"That's to be expected," said Jay with a grin. "He's a growing goose."

Gabriel crashed heavily into the gunwales, accidentally severing a line to the skysail. The crew scrambled to repair the damage, and Snipe turned to his captain. "He's a growing concern as well, sir," he said. "Seriously, how long do you intend to keep the goose on board? We really should find him a more suitable home with his own kind. He's more than doubled in size already, and if he continues to grow at this rate . . . ,"

"I know, I know! But out there . . ." said Jay, pointing toward the horizon, "out there is a merchant ship or two traveling toward us on the westerlies, and I'd like to see how Gabriel handles himself when we land that ship. From the looks of 'im, he might be useful."

Both Crossbill and Snipe looked skeptical.

"Really!" said Jay. "If not a god, that goose might just make a fine pirate. You wait and see."

AN AWKWARD GOD

In contrast to the cold, late spring, the first weeks of summer were golden ones for the crew of the *Grosbeak*. As Jay claimed to have foreseen, there was in fact a merchant ship on the horizon, a Thrushian seed hauler named the *Widgeon*. She was transporting cloth and exotic fruit and berries from the south to the colonial outposts in the Northeast. She was a three-masted carrack with a high, rounded stern and a bow that resembled the flat bill of a duck. The ship's terrified little captain, a gray-cheeked thrush named Lawrence, put up no fight when the

Grosbeak, flying the dreaded Jolly Robin, overtook him. Evidently, Blue Jay's diabolical reputation was intact, since Captain Lawrence had no doubt that Blue Jay and his crew would butcher every last one of them if they offered the slightest resistance. While the ship's hold was full of valuable cargo, it was certainly not worth losing his life or the lives of his passengers and crew.

Blue Jay, ever mindful of maintaining his fearsome image, had the giant goose stand guard over the *Widgeon*'s crew while the rest of the pirates emptied the seed hauler's

hold. Unfortunately, Gabriel's presence did not create the desired effect on the assembled captives. The poor bird looked ridiculous in his pile of patchwork clothing and his mixed-up, pimply complexion of yellow down and gray pinfeathers sticking out in all directions on his neck. He carried a sword that was much too small for him, which made it look more like a toy. Terribly uncoordinated, Gabriel tripped over the capstan and bumped his head on one of the booms. To make matters worse, the pirates' captives actually began to giggle.

Painfully aware that he was making a fool of himself, Gabriel tried to establish his authority by threatening his prisoners. "One false move . . . and I'll run you through!" he said, waving his tiny sword. This could have sounded convincing if he hadn't delivered the command in a warbling, yodel-some voice common to adolescents. "My sword is sharp, and I'm . . . I'm not afraid to use it." Then he added, "By plunder!"

His performance caused the prisoners to twitter and chuckle even more. "Did he just say 'by plunder'?" mimicked one of the prisoners under his breath. Gabriel was mortified. It was clear that the prisoners were not afraid of him in the least.

Fortunately, Blue Jay was nearby. He whirled onto the deck, looking wild, with his cutlass drawn, and confronted a black-throated warbler who had mocked Gabriel. The bird trembled before the point of Blue Jay's sword. "This one needs to be taught some manners . . . by plun-der!" he enunciated, then called, "Mr. Will's-Widow!"

"Here, sir!" answered Chuck, stepping forward with a heavy basket of grain he'd just stolen from the *Widgeon*'s hold.

"Fetch me some rope, will you?" said Jay.

"Aye, sir!" said Chuck, setting the basket down and ducking belowdecks. He soon emerged with a coil of rope slung over his shoulder.

Jay cocked his head toward the prisoner. "Now, bind this prisoner's wings behind him if you please, Chuck."

"Aye, sir!" said Chuck, lifting the bird's wings and looping the rope around them so that they stuck up together from his back like a fin.

The black-throat was mute with terror. Jay ordered Gabriel to lift the warbler up by his bound wings and dangle him over the gunwales. Gabriel hesitated at first, being of a generally sweet disposition, but Blue Jay shot him a glance as if to say, *Do it this instant!* Not wanting to fall in disfavor with his captain, the goose gingerly lifted the black-throat up by his wing tips and held him over the edge.

The warbler stared down at the earth a thousand feet below, then screeched and begged for forgiveness. "Have mercy on me! Please! Have mercy!"

Jay allowed this to go on for a bit before having Gabriel set the sailor back on deck. The sailor gasped his thanks. "Bless-you-sir-oh-God-bless-you!"

Jay looked satisfied. He knew that there would be no further trouble from the prisoners and that the incident would produce yet another story to enhance his status as a ruthless rogue. Nevertheless, before he flew away, he could not help but say to Gabriel, "Toss him overboard if he gives you more grief!"

Gabriel sheathed his sword, stood tall, crossed his wings over his chest, and glowered at the prisoners. The pirates finished emptying the *Widgeon*'s hold, leaving the crew and passengers with just enough rations to last them for a few days. Before departing, Jay could not resist the opportunity to shore up his mythic reputation. "Be grateful ya have yer lives!" he called to the *Widgeon*'s crew. "Our goose is a merciful god!" He pointed to Gabriel and then to the sky. "Be sure to tell your priests that a god is on our side now!"

Back on the *Grosbeak,* Blue Jay praised his crew and clapped the gosling on the back. "Crayee! Did you see the look on their faces when you boarded the *Widgeon*? Struck dumb, I tell you! Struck dumb by the awesome power of our young godling here! Ha-ha!"

Gabriel shuffled awkwardly from one foot to another and lowered his head as the pirates cheered him. He was both pleased and made uncomfortable by the attention, and he was a bit puzzled.

Later, while helping Junco pile up sacks of grain, Gabriel asked her, "Why did the captain call me a godling?"

"Because the Thrushians fear gods, and since your species is associated with gods," Junco explained. "Jay believes that you could be very useful to our cause."

Gabriel looked no less perplexed than before. "Um . . . what's a god exactly?"

"Ah, well, that's a puzzle," said Junco, scratching her head. "I'm not an expert on such matters, but I suppose a short answer is that a god is a large and powerful being that smaller beings tend to live in awe of. It used to be that little birds worshipped all of the larger birds — eagles, hawks, owls, and geese. As the bird colonies grew, each country chose to worship just one large bird. For instance, the Thrushians believe the owl to be the judge, jury, and executioner that rules the world. The finches in Finchland praise hawks, and tyrant birds in Tyrannida offer sacrifices to falcons and go to war in the name of eagles."

"Why?" asked Gabriel.

"I don't know. I'm not part of any country, thank the clouds!" said Junco.

"Do you have a god?" asked Gabriel.

"Not that I can name," she answered, "though I've learned to have respect for large birds, especially hawks. Crikes, those monsters come down from the sky and hit a bird and carry him off before he knows what's happened!"

"So hawks are your gods, then."

"No, no, no!" said Junco. "I avoid hawks at all costs."

"Then who rules pirates?"

Junco chuckled. "Certainly not a bird!"

Gabriel cocked his head to the side as if to say, *Then who?*

"Pirates answer to no other bird and to no other creature, but we do have a ruler of sorts."

"Who?" asked Gabriel.

"Well, the wind," she said. "The wind provides us with direction and power. Like a god, it's a little unpredictable, even moody at times. But unlike most gods, it is not confined to a country. The wind is everywhere and, inasmuch, provides us with our freedom. We pray to the wind, we read the wind, and we move with the wind."

Gabriel smiled and nodded. "I like that," he said. "I'm ruled by the wind."

Junco shook out her wings and stretched. "Well, now, more of this later. We must get back to work here." Junco began to lift her end of a sack and waited for Gabriel to lift his, but he was scratching his neck, mulling something over.

"Whose gods are geese?" he finally asked.

Junco thought for a moment, "Well, how about that? Geese don't have a country either . . . like pirates. Geese were the gods of migration, and since countries have outlawed migration, geese have very few worshippers anymore . . . only the birds that still dare to migrate." Junco lifted her end of the sack while Gabriel stood looking even more confused. "Tell you what: help me with these sacks and I'll share what I know on the subject."

Gabriel lifted his end of the heavy sack with ease, and Junco felt the weight transfer to the goose as he stacked it in the pile with little or no effort. "I'll do this," Gabriel said. "Tell me about this migration."

"All right, then," said Junco, sitting on one of the grain sacks. "A long time ago, before any colonies existed — before there were villages, for that matter — birds lived in roving communities called flocks. These flocks had no buildings, no farms, no permanent place to live. Instead of settling in one place, these flocks would travel in numbers from four to five thousand along ancient routes to nesting and feeding grounds, sleeping in trees and living off the land all along the way. Imagine that — five thousand birds, all flying together. It must have been magnificent!" Junco smiled

and sighed. "I would love to have lived back then," she said wistfully.

"Why don't birds still live in flocks?" asked Gabriel.

"Some birds still do," said Junco. "Mostly geese and ducks — because you are too large to be controlled — and any bird who chooses to be a pirate. But flocks have disappeared mainly because migration has been made illegal."

"What is this thing, *migration*?" Gabriel asked.

"Migration is the life force that urges birds to travel long distances in search of fresh feeding grounds and longer days."

"So, why wouldn't all birds still migrate?"

"Because it has been outlawed."

"Why?"

"The Thrushians who rule the land and skies have no use for migration. They figured out that they are better able to control their subjects and their food supply if they can keep them in one place. So they set up farms and workshops and villages for non-thrush birds such as sparrows and warblers to work and live. They force the poor villagers to give half of what they produce to the colony. To help convince them, Thrushia has adopted a bird-god that frightens small birds into staying put."

"Which bird is that?" said Gabriel.

"The white owl, or ghost owl," said Junco. "According to the Thrushian priests, the white owl knows which subjects are disloyal and which ones try to leave the colony. It is said that the owls will hunt and kill the traitors in the dead of night; the owl swallows the poor sots whole, sucks out their souls, then spits out the bones and feathers in messy little bundles called pellets. The whole thing is disgusting — and poor birds are living every day in fear and poverty when they should be flying free!"

Gabriel's eyes were wide with terror.

"Don't worry, owls are unlikely to attack a goose," said Junco, "even if he is a low-down pirate like you!" She lifted her side of another grain sack. "Now then, put that sack on the pile, or we'll feel the wrath of the god of grain!"

"Who is that?" asked Gabriel.

"My stomach," Junco joked. "A very powerful god!"

"I know that god!" Gabriel laughed, piling the last sack in the hold. "I'm more than glad to serve my stomach!"

6

THE DOLDRUMS

Come, messmates, pass the grog around

For our time is short together,

For our hearts must stop, STOP!

And our spirits drop, DROP!

At the first sign of cold weather.

For tonight we'll merry, merry be,

For tonight we'll merry, merry be,

For tonight we'll merry, merry be,

For we are birds of a feather.

The days following the *Grosbeak*'s encounter with the *Widgeon* were sweet ones, indeed. Jay knew there would be retribution by the colonials for plundering their ships, and there was still the worry of the crows in the forest below. But for the time being, the crew was feeling generally happy and content with fair weather and plenty of food to fill their bellies. They set to the routine tasks on board with renewed enthusiasm. They mended sails and attended to the countless other repairs and maintenance a ship requires. Gabriel made himself useful wherever he could. In addition to being able to lift a grain sack out of the hold by simply reaching down with his long neck and grabbing it with his bill, he was also particularly adept at adjusting the rigging.

There was also a fair amount of leisure time on the *Grosbeak*. The crew spent quite a bit of time knitting, sewing, and weaving. They made their own clothes, storage containers, and lanterns lit by lightning bugs. Gabriel sported a red cap, expertly knitted by none other than Chuck-Will's-Widow.

The crew would also amuse themselves by telling stories, playing music, and singing (if you could call it that) throughout the day and often far into the night.

> *Dirty Sailor Robin was fatter than his nest.*
> *He wore it like his breeches,*
> > *filled with all his "past."*
> *The nest 'twas full o' buggots,*
> > *all dancin' in a line.*
> *Before the music started,*
> *They'd eaten his behind.*

Other verses of this song featured more unfortunate birds such as Popeye Plover, Sore-Throated Grackle, Green Little Bluebird, and any other miscreant that inspired song. The songs "Rats 'n' Bats 'n' Fisher Cats" and "Birdskuller Bill" were other favorites with the pirates. These songs — or fragments of them — continue to be sung to this day by birds in backyards and forests all around the world. It's the rare bird who doesn't know that they were originally sung by pirates.

The camaraderie and good humor lasted for about a month. But the pirates' need to plunder and their thirst for adventure couldn't stay dormant for long. Because it was late summer and harvesttime was still weeks away, shipping traffic was light with the exception of the Thrushian warships that constantly patrolled the borders. With nothing to do, the pirates became restless and bored. They didn't know where they were bound. Worse, Jay didn't seem to know either. Nearly every day he announced that they were just upwind of some treasure ship or a few nautical miles away from some grand adventure, but none materialized. As the crew grew increasingly antsy, the singing and storytelling became scarcer until it finally stopped altogether.

Instead, grumbling and gossip bubbled up in the dark, secluded corners of the ship:

"I'm afraid our fine captain's lost his bearings for good this time. Must've gotten a blow on the noggin from that clumsy goose. Cracked his compass, if you know what I mean."

"Mr. Crossbill looks more cross every time he visits wi' the captain. It's plain as print he ain't happy with our little predicament here. Yellow Belly here says he heard Crossbill arguing with the captain from outside his cabin."

"That goose thar has an appetite, to be sure. A growing concern . . . if you know what I mean. Have ye noticed that we're flying lower and lower in the sky as that boy gets bigger?"

"All's we do is feed that goose! We fill up the hold every morning, and the food is gone in no time!"

"He's insatiable, I tell you!"

It was true that Gabriel was growing remarkably, but

not unusually, fast. Not for a goose. It would take about three more months for Gabriel to reach his full size and weight. Then he would weigh ten to fourteen pounds, the equivalent of sixty-four blue jays, and he would have a wingspan of five feet, nearly the length of the *Grosbeak*!

Unfortunately, Gabriel was still weeks away from fledging. Most of the pirates felt that the goose would have to go sooner or later. However, most of them were also very fond of Gabriel and didn't mind caring for him till he was able to strike out on his own. Others wanted to leave him in the care of other geese and let his own kind take care of him. Some simply wanted to rid themselves of the goose, no matter where or when, to let him fend for himself.

One particularly hot day, Junco overheard Blackcap grousing to Thrasher, "That young goose needs to fledge, I tell you, or he'll never leave! Why don't we just tip him overboard, much the way my mother pushed me out of the nest!"

"That'll teach him to fly quick enough," said Thrasher.

"He can hold his own. Why should we be spottin'

'im?" said Blackcap. "He can fly. . . . He just needs a little encouragement, if you know what I mean."

"He just needs a little push," said Thrasher. "Tip him over, I say."

So enraged by what she heard, Junco flew at Thrasher and slammed into his back. Thrasher toppled to the deck. Junco pecked his head between curses. "I'll topple every last one of you!"

Blackcap was trying to pry Junco off Thrasher when Snipe appeared. "Stand off!" he ordered. That ended the fight.

"What's goin' on here?" he demanded. "Junco, what's this about?"

Junco said nothing. Thrasher and Blackcap were silent, too. Snipe knew what the dispute was about and did not press the matter, but he reported the incident to Jay.

"The crew is openly fighting over the goose, Captain," said Snipe. "It's time to make a decision about Gabriel, or I'm afraid there will be trouble."

Jay had begun to worry that if circumstances didn't change for the better and soon, he might just have a mutiny on his hands. This was not implausible, as it had already happened to him six times — twice on the *Grosbeak* alone and four times on other ships, each the result of a lack of enthusiasm by the crew for what they called "far-fetched harebrained schemes" by Captain Blue Jay, not unlike raising a goose on board his ship, for example. The fact that Blue Jay had survived six mutinies only enhanced his legend in the world of bird pirates. Still, mutiny was a demoralizing experience for all involved, and Jay wanted very much to avoid a seventh.

"Mr. Crossbill!" said Jay.

"Yes, sir?"

"Set us a course for Oak's Eye Cay."

"Oak's Eye Cay! Yes, sir!" said Crossbill. "What course, sir?"

"Southeast. Should be less than two days."

"True, Captain," said Crossbill, "but southeast?"

"It will be the shortest route. I sense the crew needs a bit of a diversion, a little of the old R 'n' R and right quick, if you know what I mean. We can spend a couple of days on Oak's Eye, gather some supplies, and plan our next excursion."

"Yes, sir. I understand," said Crossbill. "My concern is with the wind. We have a steady stream here. We'll have to lower altitude to fly southeast, and it's bound to be breezy to nothing down below the airstream."

"Aye, but the ship's nearly empty and so can take full advantage of whatever wind there is," said Jay. "Let's take her down and put her under full sail. If need be, we'll kedge a bit here and there."

"Aye, but if I may . . ." said Crossbill, who was always a bit formal in his speech.

"Speak freely, Crossbill!" said Blue Jay.

"What about your cousin?" said Crossbill.

"Teach?" said Jay. "Aye, he's been more trouble than usual of late, hasn't he?"

Teach was the leader of the notorious Crows of Black Point. They were pirates who preferred attacking ships from the ground in heavily armed swarms that overwhelmed most of the ships they targeted. Usually the crows were satisfied to empty the ships of their cargo and send them on their way. But of late, Teach and his cronies had been commandeering entire ships and murdering or marooning the crew. This ruthless behavior was considered dishonorable by most pirates, who generally spared the crew of any ship they plundered and left them with enough provisions to sustain themselves until they reached the nearest port. Murdering and marooning any sailor without just cause was despicable, and it seemed that Teach had taken to doing just that. To make matters worse, as a corvid, Teach was also a not-too-distant cousin of Blue Jay.

"Teach has been harassing pirate ships as well," said Snipe. "It's said that he has twenty-four ships in a single tree at Black Point and that eight of them had flown black flags."

"Ha!" Jay laughed. "Teach is me cousin, and while he and I have been rivals since we were fledglings, he would not dare attack my ship. He may harass us a bit, flying so close to the forest, but look down there." Jay pointed down toward the main deck, where Gabriel sat alone with Junco.

Jay continued: "I have no desire to see my cousin under any circumstance, but if we do, won't it be grand to see Teach's expression when he comes face-to-face with our Gabriel there?"

"He might think twice about boarding our ship," agreed Crossbill.

"So, Bill, shall we sail to Oak's Eye?" asked Blue Jay.

"Aye, sir! Due south it is," said Crossbill. "To Oak's Eye!"

Oak's Eye Cay was a safe haven for pirates in what was becoming a world of inhospitable colonial ports. Oak's Eye was a green island atop a towering cliff, surrounded by an ocean of ancient pine trees that was known as the

Oak's Eye Cay

Glitter Cavern

← Spy

Handle

The Ladle

Great Northeast Forest, or Paxwood. The eastern face of the cay was a semicircular cliff rising four hundred feet over the forest, topped by a dense stand of wide oaks. The pirates could see for miles from this vantage point. The cay resembled a gigantic tree stump with a grove of trees growing on the cut. The western face sloped gently toward Paxwood Forest and was covered by trees that surrounded a small pond about halfway down the mountain slope. On the eastern side of the pond, hidden behind a bramble, was a tunnel, a passageway to the Glitter Cavern at the heart of the cliff. This vast, hollow vault contained a large subterranean lake. Two passageways connected the main cavern: one in the east named Spy and one in the west named Handle. These provided illumination to Glitter Cavern, which was a sight to behold on sunny mornings and afternoons. The cavern would sparkle with golden light reflecting off the surface of the lake. Hence the name Glitter Cavern. The illumination of the cavern was so spectacular that it led to the common belief that there was a fortune in treasure, gold, and jewels at the bottom of the lake. Of course, no birds, not even ducks or loons, had ever proved this. If there was treasure there, it remained out of the reach of birds, even swimming and diving birds.

The light often created two spectacular effects. In the morning, light would stream through Spy, bounce around the cavern, and slip out of Handle, lighting the small pond on the western side named the Ladle. On these mornings, The Ladle looked like a giant bowl of glowing soup, complete with steam as the fog lifted from its surface. It was considered an enchanted pool by most animals, who avoided it. The pirates, of course, knew better. The second phenomenon was even more awe-inspiring. At sunset, with a pink or red sky in the background, the light would stream out of Spy on the dark eastern side of the cay and project over the forest. This light in the middle of the dark cliff side was known as the Oak's Eye. It could be seen for miles burning red-orange and gold in the center of the dark mountains.

Both the cavern and pond were guarded by an ancient turtle named Snapper. He was over three feet long and said to be more than one hundred years old. No one dared to get too close to the water for fear of being snapped by Snapper. No one, that is, save Blue Jay, who was one of his best friends and would spend hours sharing stories with the old turtle.

The crew of the *Grosbeak* was cheered by the news that they were sailing to Oak's Eye Cay. They eagerly settled into their tasks. For the time being, contentment had been restored to the ship. Oak's Eye Cay was two days away under the best conditions. Unfortunately, the *Grosbeak* and her crew weren't going to experience the best of anything for quite some time.

SHIPWRECKED!

Down upon the forest floor,
Don't fall asleep upon the leaves.
The ground is where we go to die,
Strangled by a noose of soil.

Heave away, mates! Heeeeeave!" croaked Snipe, as he and the rest of the crew strained at their kedging lines to pull their ship skyward. It was the tenth day since the *Grosbeak* had begun its two-day journey to Oak's Eye Cay, and nothing, absolutely nothing, had been going according to Blue Jay's plan. Crossbill's concern about the southerly route had been correct. The cool breezes that blew from the north were light and inconsistent. Adding to the frustration, the west wind overhead began to build and carried a tantalizing stream of merchant ships, flying well above them. Unfortunately, the *Grosbeak*'s speed and altitude made it nearly impossible for the pirates to gain any advantage on the passing ships.

Finally, Jay could stand the temptation no longer and abruptly ordered a change in course. "Crossbill! Snipe!" he called. "Prepare the crew to kedge. We're heading east to chase some ships for a spell."

Kedging was an exhausting task. Each of the crew had to don a kedging harness, which was attached to the gunwales of the ship. The kedgers would then fly with all their might, pulling the ship through the sky and hoping to stumble upon an airstream. If there was no wind to be found, then kedging was again employed to "hammock" the ship in the trees below, where they would wait for a decent wind. Hammocking involved bringing the ship to a safe location between strong trees and tying it off, a maneuver that was tricky and dangerous. A miscalculation could end in shipwreck. Blue Jay had been forced to hammock his ship the night before in a part of the forest that happened to be inhabited by a very large horned owl who seemed to take great pleasure in harassing the pirates throughout the night. The silent devil tried to attack any bird who moved on the open deck, forcing the entire crew, including Gabriel, to squeeze together belowdecks as far away from any opening as possible since the owl could

easily grab a pirate through a hatch or porthole. It was an experience that none of the crew was eager to repeat, especially Jay.

"Just a bit of a detour," Jay said to encourage the kedgers. "If we raise the ship to the air current above, we'll chase down a couple of ships and be in Oak's Eye for the weekend." The crew was uninspired by their captain's words. Exhausted from the night before, they pulled the ship in jerks prompted by Snipe's commands. "Heave away, mates! We're almost there! Heeeeave!"

Finally they reached what they thought was the western airstream. The sails filled, and the ship began to move forward at a considerable speed. The exhausted crew removed their kedging harnesses, but the airstream turned out to be nothing more than a sustained gust. The ship made progress, then lost wind completely and began to drop rapidly from the sky.

"Ye fickle witch!" Jay screamed, swinging his sword at the sky. "Fickle, fickle witch!"

Urgently, Crossbill asked if he should order the crew to hammock the ship.

"Aye, blast it!" Jay was in a full rage now and continued to curse and stab at the sky.

"Prepare to hammock!" Crossbill called from his perch.

"Get those kedging harnesses back on!" shouted Snipe. "Step smartly now!"

The frightened crew moved as quickly as they could, but the ship's descent was too rapid. By the time some of the crew had donned their kedging harnesses, the ship's hull was scraping the treetops. It was a terrifying sound, like giant claws ripping at the belly of the ship. As she strapped on her harness, Junco looked over toward Gabriel. Unable to help with the kedging, the poor goose was standing alone, looking completely helpless and terrified. The sight of Gabriel filled Junco's heart with sadness as she realized for the first time that perhaps she had been selfish in keeping the goose on board.

"Just hang on, Gabriel!" Junco called to him.

There was a sudden *CRACK* as a sharp branch pushed through the hull, and the *Grosbeak* listed violently to the port side, throwing the crew against the railing and over the edge, still attached to their kedging lines. There was general mayhem as the pirates scrambled over one another to get back in position. Junco untangled herself from Blackcap's line and glanced over toward Gabriel.

"HEAVE AWAY!" barked Snipe over the desperate cries of the crew.

Junco glanced at the spot where Gabriel had stood moments ago. The goose was gone!

"GABRIEL!" shouted Junco. "He's fallen!"

Snipe shouted, "Heave away!" and the kedgers flew skyward with all their might, but even without the weight of the goose, they were barely able to lift the ship above the branches.

"GABRIEL!" Junco cried, but could not be heard over the din.

Though he had not witnessed the goose's fall, Blue Jay could see Junco's distress and realized that Gabriel had been lost.

The kedgers screamed as they strained at their lines.

"That's it, mates!" Crossbill encouraged. "It's working!"

"What is that cursed bird doing?" roared Snipe, pointing toward Junco, who stood motionless on deck. "JUNCO! HEAVE! DAMN YOU!"

Junco did not so much as look up. Instead she defiantly unbuckled her harness, threw it on deck, and flew from the ship.

"DESERTER!" yelled Snipe. "I swear I'll hang you myself when I catch you!"

The ship had lifted above the trees, and the sails briefly filled but then fell limp, as they were nowhere near the airstream.

Once again the air had defeated them, and Jay turned to Crossbill and said with a simmering rage, "There is no wind here. Let's find a place to hammock before these birds die from exhaustion!"

The two pirates quickly scanned the dense canopy of pine below them, desperately searching for an opening where they could suspend the ship. The light was beginning to fade, and the forest appeared to be a solid mass of blue-green with no openings in sight. Then Crossbill pointed to the west. "There, sir! Dead ahead," he said ominously. "Black Point!" It appeared as a sharp black hole cut out of an undulating sea of trees.

"Black Point," Jay repeated. "Cryee!" Jay searched quickly for another option, and seeing none he shook his head. "Tell Snipe to bring her down. We have no choice but to hammock there."

"But sir, the crows!" Crossbill said warily.

"We have no choice, Bill!" said Jay irritably. "There is no wind. Now go! Quickly, before it's too late."

Hammocking was never a simple matter and was ideally

attempted with a strong, well-rested crew. Despite promptings from Snipe, Crossbill, and Jay, the ship began to fall.

"HEAVE, MATES! HEEEAVE!"

The kedgers strained at their lines, trying desperately to regain control of the ship.

"HEEEEAVE!"

Kedgers began to drop from the sky. Some hung unconscious at the end of their lines. Others cut their own lines and deserted their posts.

"HEEEEAVE!"

Suddenly, the world was filled with the deafening sound of branches and yardarms cracking and by the terrified cries of shipmates as the ship crashed. When the ship finally came to rest in the limbs of a giant pine deep within the canopy of the forest, deadly quiet followed for a few moments before the groans of the wounded could be heard.

The *Grosbeak* was wrecked, its sails, rigging, and part

of a yardarm drooping from the pine branches. Many of the crew lay strewn about the deck, stunned or knocked senseless. Others, still attached to their kedging lines, swung helplessly from the rigging. Blue Jay flew around the ship, assessing the damage and providing encouragement. "Don't fret, mates. We'll have you mended in a moment!" In a flurry, he gathered on deck what able crew members were left and, with the help of Crossbill and Snipe, dispatched them to do a head count. "Come on, now. The light is wasting. We have no time to lose."

Finally, Snipe informed the captain that there were nine dead, twenty-one injured, and seven unaccounted for, including Gabriel and "the deserter" Junco.

"Sticky pitch! Snipe, put together a search party. I want to find as many of the lost as we can before nightfall!"

"Aye, sir!" said Snipe.

"And, Snipe?" said Jay.

"Sir?"

"No matter what has happened to him, I want Gabriel to be found."

Snipe bristled at this. "Sir, if I may say, I find it very unlikely that the goose survived the fall. What is more, we've traveled a considerable distance from the point at which we lost him. It will take hours. . . ."

"Cryee, Snipe!" said Jay. "If he's alive, then we will rescue him. If we don't, then it is unlikely he or we will survive the predators in the forest tonight. I want him found! Am I understood?"

"Aye, sir!" said the quartermaster obediently.

"And, Snipe?" said Jay.

"Yes, Captain?"

"I expect that you will find that Junco is with Gabriel," said Jay. "I realize that she deserted the ship, but I want you to leave her punishment to me."

Snipe nodded without a word and proceeded to organize a search party.

"Crossbill?" called Jay.

"Aye, sir?"

"Have Creeper and a few of the riggers prepare funeral nests for the dead," said Jay. "I want to lay them to rest properly."

"Aye, sir!"

Jay scanned the trees warily for any sign of crows. He spied two wood thrushes perched timidly in a nearby tree and called to them. "Ho there! Can you give us help here? I have wounded in need of a physician."

The thrushes did not respond. "I said we need a—"

A loud, sharp *"CAW!"* came from some nearby trees, and the thrushes quickly disappeared. All activity stopped on board as the crew's attention was fixed on the forest around them.

"Crows!" growled Snipe.

"Can you see them?" whispered Crossbill.

Jay had sharp eyes, but neither he nor the other pirates

could see the crows. Then came another *"CAW,"* still invisible but closer than the first.

In a hushed but determined voice, Jay said to Crossbill and Snipe, "Quietly instruct the crew to go below and arm themselves, then await my order!"

"CAW! CAW! CAW! CAW!" Suddenly the entire forest filled with the raucous sound as a mob of crows settled into the trees surrounding the *Grosbeak*.

8

FISHER'S PREY

Gabriel lay on the forest floor, where he had managed
to bury himself deep in a pile of leaves and pine needles
after falling from the faltering *Grosbeak*. He had watched
as the ship limped away through the sky, deaf to his cries
of distress, and he was unable to take wing and fly after
them. He was alone in the gathering darkness of a strange
forest. Trees rose, like tall black columns, into a greater
darkness above. His body was cracked, bruised, and
bloodied. Gabriel knew from the pirates' stories that there
were mammals in the forest who would be on the prowl
for an easy meal such as himself. He could already hear

their growls and screams echo through the forest. Only the scent of pine disguised him from predators. He harbored a horrible fear that he would never make it through the night. He shuddered, closed his eyes, and sobbed. Eventually he fell into an exhausted, fitful sleep.

Deep inside his makeshift nest, Gabriel was startled awake in the middle of the night and hissed in defense. Then he raised his head and listened intently. Out of the darkness came sounds, the echoes of indiscernible voices as well as cracks and groans.

Finally, he made out a faint "Gaaabrielll! Gaaabrielll!" Then again, "Gaaabrielll!" That was Junco's voice! Gabriel's heart filled with hope, and he opened his beak to call out in answer. But a low, rattling growl from quite nearby sent a chill through him, and he clamped his mouth shut. He waited in silence.

Finally, when he could stand it no longer, Gabriel poked his beak carefully through the pine needles to get a sense of what was out there. He could only make out vague forms of trees and underbrush. He was about to stick his neck out a bit farther for a better look when a large, snarling creature jumped onto the ground directly in front of his hiding place.

Gabriel shuddered at the sight of the mammal. It was muscular, shaped like a mink or weasel, but four times as big, with long, dark fur, sharp claws, and glowing red eyes. It was a fisher cat, one of the most vicious hunters in the forest, a merciless predator that pounced on and killed prey with the speed of a hawk. Fishers would attack and consume most anything, even animals bigger than themselves, but they were particularly fond of birds.

To Gabriel's relief, the creature seemed to be either unaware of his presence or else distracted by something else in the forest. Then Junco's call came again. "Gabriel!" The fisher growled and crouched low to the ground.

No! thought Gabriel. *Junco, no! Go away! Leave me here!*

Just then Junco flew into view, a small flash of gray in the darkness. The fisher tensed and quivered in anticipation of the kill. Gabriel gathered all of his strength and will, shot out of his hiding place, and clamped his beak down hard on the fisher's hind leg. The fisher gave a piercing scream, then whipped around, nearly folding itself in half, and attacked the goose with a flurry of teeth and claws. Gabriel was overwhelmed by the ferocity of the fisher's assault but held on with all his might. *Fool,* he said to himself. *You attacked without a plan. Now what will you do?*

As if in answer, Junco yelled, "Let go, Gabriel! Roll! Roll away now, Gabriel!" Brandishing a cutlass in each wing, Junco swooped down and landed on the fisher's head. Then she raised her swords and plunged them into the creature's eyes. The fisher let out a blood-curdling scream before Junco silenced the predator for good with a sweep of her blade to its throat. At this, Gabriel fainted.

9

TEACH'S MOB

CAW! CAW! CAW CAW!" the crows chanted as they
perched in the trees that surrounded the *Grosbeak*. Then,
as if on cue, the caws stopped abruptly, and the crows
began to murmur like an eager theater audience waiting for
the curtain to rise at a play.

Jay cleared his throat and, in a perfect crow dialect said,
"Hear me, corvid cousins. As you can see, we have wrecked
our ship and have many dead and wounded. We need your
help!" No response other than some excited murmuring.
Jay tried again. "A word with Teach if he's amongst you!"
he shouted.

Jay could not stand the thought of asking Teach for
assistance. Teach was a robber, a weapons dealer, a

murderer, but he was also the leader of a mob of more than one hundred crows that had the means and might to help them out of their predicament. Still, Teach had no allegiances to anything or anybody except his own power and wealth. He would steal from or deal with colonials, peasants, pirates — anyone who had something of value to him. Teach was brilliant and treacherous, ruthless in battle, and seemed to have intimidated the colonial government, which, for some reason Jay couldn't puzzle out, turned a blind eye on the crow's behavior.

Jay called up to the crows again. "I wish to speak with Teach!"

Jay was startled by a familiar voice, answering nearby and right behind him. "Aw, Blue Jay!" Teach drawled. "This is certainly a surprise!"

Jay spun around to see three large crows, dressed entirely in black, emerging from the hatch right there on the *Grosbeak:* Teach, Teach's brother Bellamy, and Teach's first mate, Avery.

TEACH

Teach wore a long coat and a tall, wide-brimmed hat. His feet were festooned with gold rings, and in one wing he held an elaborate switch with multiple blades that curved and twisted like silver flames. From the sharp smile on his well-shined beak to the cold light that burned in his eyes, Teach wore an attitude of cruel amusement. The crows in the trees clacked their bills in approval at their leader's dramatic entrance.

"Well, now," said Jay. "Look who's here! How did you happen to get inside my ship, Teach?"

"Your *ship?* It resembles more a pile of sticks, I'd say," the crow said, mocking. "You know, y'all have a rather large hole in the bottom of it, large enough for three to fly right in, our wings fully extended!"

"Yes?" said Blue Jay, sounding annoyed. "We've wrecked here!"

"Aw, you mean you're only here by accident? Why, I thought you'd come by to visit your cousin," said Teach sarcastically. "You know, you never visit anymore!"

"I don't have time for this, Teach!" said Jay. "I have dead and wounded crew to attend to and a ship to repair."

"Aw, Blue Jay, Blue Jay, this just won't do! First you drop into the neighborhood without a word of notice. On top of that, your ship appears to carry no gifts whatsoever for your long-lost cousins. Downright uncivilized, if you ask me!" The crows in the trees applauded in agreement. "Tsk! Tsk! What do you have to say for yourself?"

Normally, Jay tried to approach his insane relative calmly and with caution. This time his rage got the better of him. "I'll tell you what I have to say, cousin. I say I am in very bad humor tonight and not at all in the mood for your tricks and mockery. My crew here have done some hard fightin', seen some hard weather, and felt a hard landing! We're not bearin' gifts because, no offense to you, we weren't coming for a visit! We were merely passing by, lost our wind, and landed in your tree here. We ain't askin' for trouble; we're askin' for your help. If you don't want to help, then I'm askin' you to leave us in peace so that we can get our ship outta your stinkin' trees. So either lend us your help or get out of our way, cousin!"

Maintaining his cool composure, Teach said, "Aw, Jay, you know I don't like to feud with my relations. Of course, you and your crew may leave in peace." He paused and poked the deck with his blade. "The ship, on the other hand, you'll leave here. Think of it as payment for damages to . . . my *stinkin'* trees."

"You'll not take our ship without a fight!" cried Jay, drawing his sword.

With blazing speed, Teach whirled the switch over his shoulder and, in two swift movements, knocked Jay's sword out of his right wing and clipped the wing feathers on his left. Bits of brilliant blue flight feathers swirled in spirals toward the deck. Teach glanced at the feathers and grinned, all the while pointing the blade of his switch at Jay's throat. Then he called to the furious and bewildered *Grosbeak* crew around him, "Make one move . . . ah say, one move, and I'll cut his head off as well."

Jay was still and defiant. "What now, Teach?"

Teach's smile widened as his eyes darkened. "Bellamy! Watch him!"

Calmly, Teach impaled one of Jay's lost feathers onto the silver blade of his switch with an audible *crunch* and inspected it. "What now?" Teach repeated. He gave a signal, and one hundred crows drew their swords in a single resounding, cold metallic echo. Teach smiled with great satisfaction.

10

BRIARLOCH

It was midmorning of the next day when Gabriel finally awoke and was surprised to find himself covered in a dense blanket of pine needles with only the tip of his bill exposed. He was overjoyed to find Junco napping beside him, her head resting on the hilt of her sword.

"Junco?" Gabriel said weakly.

Junco jerked awake. "Gabriel!" she cried, hopping to her feet. "How are you feeling?"

"I'm just fine — owww!" groaned Gabriel.

Junco inspected the goose. "Let's have a look at you now." Gabriel's head and neck were covered with a horrible crisscross of cuts and scrapes, and his beak was notched but not broken.

Junco grimaced. "I'd say that you came out of that remarkably well. I mean, given that you're not dead!"

Gabriel laughed weakly. "Thanks to you."

"Yes, well, I think we both managed to save each other's skin last night," said Junco. "If you hadn't grabbed that monster's leg, I would have been a goner myself."

"Where is . . . ?" said Gabriel, lifting his head painfully.

Junco pointed to a large mound of pine needles nearby. "I covered it over so that its mates don't get a whiff if they start searching for their comrade." She scanned the trees above as she talked. "What's more, this forest is full of predators! I hate to say it, but we should try to get away from here soon . . . if you're up for it."

"To the ship?" asked Gabriel. "Where is the *Grosbeak*?"

"Hopefully hammocked somewhere not too far east of here," said Junco. "I doubt we'd catch up to the *Grosbeak* today, especially with you in your present condition, but

I know a place along the way where we might be able to scrounge some food and hole up for the night."

"Where?" asked Gabriel.

"It's a little sparrow village nearby called Briarloch," said Junco. "Can you walk, Gabriel?"

After a couple of tries, the poor gosling struggled to his feet and tottered around in an unsteady circle. "Lead the way," he said with groggy resolve.

Sparrows tended to be territorial and clannish, not the ideal bird to look to in a time of need. But seeking shelter in Briarloch was Junco and Gabriel's best hope of safety.

As they plodded along, Junco worried about how they would defend themselves if they encountered another fisher cat or, worse, a mob of crows. At first the forest was filled with the sounds of other birds singing their identifiable songs to one another: warblers with their high-pitched squeaks, finches and their complex twittering, and woodpeckers with their song that sounded so much like laughter. They were singing, "I am here! I am here!" as was the custom with birds in the forest to indicate that all was well. As long as the birds were singing, Junco knew that there was no imminent danger. But when the songs changed to warning calls—*"CHIP! CHIP! CHIP!"*—Junco grew uneasy. Just out of the corner of her eye, she could glimpse gray-brown birds shadowing them at a safe distance. She realized that the warning calls were directed at Gabriel and herself.

"Ah, sparrows, they're not the friendliest bunch," Junco said to Gabriel. "We must be getting close to Briarloch."

Junco and Gabriel eventually came across a small group of the birds scratching a field into the hard-packed soil.

Sparrows were trade folk and farmers, hard workers with most of their labor devoted to the gathering and storage of seed. Junco approached them, intending to ask for directions to the village.

"Helloo," she called to the farmers, but there was no acknowledgment. "Hello?" she called again, and stepped closer. As one, the reticent sparrows flew to the trees, where they perched and cautiously looked down on the strangers. "Come on, Gabriel," said Junco. "There's no point. We'll find Briarloch on our own."

"Why wouldn't they talk to us?" asked Gabriel as they walked on.

"Because they're afraid," said Junco.

"Afraid of what?" asked Gabriel.

"Afraid of everything!" said Junco in an exasperated tone.

They walked on for quite a while, and Junco noticed that Gabriel's pace was slowing down considerably.

"It's just a bit farther, I promise," said Junco. "I'm afraid that I'm not used to calculating distances on foot. . . ."

Gabriel laughed at this. "Well, you saved my life and slew a fisher cat . . . We can't be good at everything!"

She could tell that the goose was in pain from the beating the night before, yet he kept moving forward without uttering a word of complaint.

~~~~~

When they finally reached the stream that led to Briarloch, Gabriel visibly perked up. The sight of water always seemed to excite the goose. Junco had noticed that whenever the *Grosbeak* sailed over a river or lake, Gabriel would stop whatever he was doing and stare longingly out at the water.

"I have an idea," said Junco. "Why don't you swim to Briarloch? That way I could fly ahead. It would be much safer for both of us than trudging along on the ground here."

Gabriel stopped in his tracks. He wanted nothing more, but the truth was that he had never been swimming before. He had occasionally drunk and bathed at the shore of a lake or pond, after being lowered by his shipmates on a tarsus, then hauled up again. But he had never gone for an actual swim in his life!

"Go ahead in," said Junco with a smile. "It'll be good for you. Besides, I'm not certain how the sparrows will react to a goose at the gates of Briarloch. You can swim in the pond for a bit, and I'll come fetch you later."

Gabriel hesitated. "I don't know," he said. "What if . . . there's trouble?"

"Trouble? Ha!" said Junco. "There won't be any trouble. These sparrows are peaceful. Now, go on. Get in the water!"

Gabriel enthusiastically shed his jacket and frock, folded them neatly, and placed them on his back between his wings. And with a smile, he waddled into the water. He looked ridiculously happy, still wearing his hat and breeches as he swam in awkward, noisy surges toward the middle of the stream. Junco flew next to him, providing words of encouragement. "You're doing a splendid job! Now, stay in the middle of the stream if you can. You want to avoid any turtles that might be hiding in the shallows. Well done!"

Gabriel seemed pleased with himself as he paddled along noisily. Junco was nervous about attracting the attention of a fisher or some other hungry, opportunistic mammal. The stream was narrow, its high dirt banks topped with spindly gray birch trees that leaned precariously toward the middle of the stream, their sun-starved leaves casting a yellow reflection on the water below. The branches provided perfect hiding places for predators that could easily pounce on them from above.

"Shhh!" Junco whispered to Gabriel. "Swim as quietly as you can, for I fear we're being watched." Gabriel tried to smooth out his paddling, but his inexperienced feet kept sloshing noisily with each stroke.

Shooplop! Shooplop! Shooplop!

As Gabriel paddled downstream, Junco could sense that they were being followed. The shadows that moved within the shadows around them were the same sparrows they had seen earlier, and her heart was filled with both rage and pity for the fearful birds.

Eventually, the stream widened into a dark pond that presented Briarloch on the opposite shore.

"Where is it?" asked Gabriel. "I don't see anything."

"Straight ahead," said Junco, pointing across the pond. "See that immense tangle of brambles yonder?"

Gabriel nodded.

"That, my friend, is Briarloch," said Junco, landing on the goose's back. "Listen, Gabriel. I'm going to go speak with these sparrows now, so I'd like you to swim toward the middle of the pond and stay there till I send word. Do you understand?"

"But why?" said Gabriel. "I thought you said they were peaceful."

"Well, they are . . . They're just a bit standoffish," said Junco. "I'll be fine. Just keep an eye out for me, will you?" And with that, she flew off, leaving Gabriel looking worried.

Junco approached the swirling wall of brambles and thorns that fortified Briarloch. There was no obvious entrance to the village, so Junco flew into the nearest opening. She was immediately set on by a pair of sparrows wielding crude wooden spears. One was wearing a straw hat with no brim and a jacket with gray and brown horizontal stripes. "Now halt! Halt now! Name yer state and purpose!" he said. "I mean, state yer name and purpose!" Junco hovered a respectful distance away from the guards.

"He said, state yer purpose!" snapped the second sparrow.

Junco held up her feet as a gesture of peace. "I am called Junco. That goose over there and I were attacked by a fisher last night. We seek a place to rest till we are able to continue our journey." The sparrows' eyes widened when they spotted the giant goose. Seeing Junco threatened at spear point, Gabriel rushed madly toward them, his red cap cocked to one side and an angry, determined expression on his face.

"Hold, Gabriel!" Junco called. "There's no trouble here." Gabriel slowed and stopped beside Junco. Junco hopped onto his back and patted his neck. "These young birds are here to escort me to the appropriate village elder, aren't you?" Terrified, the sparrows bobbed their heads in wide-eyed agreement.

Accompanied by the two sentries, Junco flew through the village of Briarloch, all the while admiring the surprising craftsmanship displayed in the sparrows' dwellings. Residences were decorated with woven plant and floral designs. The Seed Hall bore a mural, woven entirely of sticks, of sparrows harvesting and storing seed. The facade of the tavern had an elaborate image of a laughing, oafish fox sharing drinks with a gang of birds. The tavern's entryway was located in the middle of the fox's chest, where his heart would be. The tavern itself was a large open hall filled with perches, feeding stations, and ropes strung from wall to wall. Light poured through hundreds of small windows in crisscrossing shafts of light. It being morning, the tavern was nearly empty.

"Covey? Cyrus?" called a friendly voice. "You boys are a bit late for breakfast, but come down and I'll fix somethin' for you."

"We have a visitor here to see you, Poppa," one of the sparrows called back.

With a flutter of wings, the few patrons lurking in the dark corners of the tavern repositioned themselves. Junco touched the hilt of her sword lightly.

"Poppa?" called Cyrus.

"Well, don't just stand there," called the voice. "Bring this visitor down!"

The group flew down to a pile of grain sacks and baskets. In their midst stood the fattest sparrow Junco had ever seen. His face was puffed and pinched, with crescent eyes. He wore a rust-colored skullcap on his head with a matching sash over gray breeches. He had only one leg and hopped toward them with the aid of a wooden peg. He squinted at Junco warily for a moment from behind small rectangular glasses. Then he chuckled. "Well, well. Welcome, miss. Pardon my manners. We don't receive many visitors here, not these days!" The sparrow held his right wing out to Junco. "I'm Poppa Fox."

Poppa Fox was village elder, innkeeper, country doc-
tor, and teacher, and his tavern, the Sooty Fox, was the
hub of the village. Nearly every bird in Briarloch spent
part of the week helping out at the tavern, though Poppa
Fox generally favored hiring sparrows unable to gather
food on their own or defend themselves adequately: the
very young, the very old, or the injured.

Junco introduced herself in turn, then went straight

to the point. "My goose out there needs attention. He took a beating from a fisher last night."

Poppa Fox frowned and smoothed the feathers under his chin. "Hmmm. Your goose . . . and a fisher?" He examined Junco's face. "No offense, but you look as if you had a rough night as well."

Junco grimaced. "Yes, the fisher doled out plenty for the both of us."

"And what, pray tell, is the present condition of this fisher?" Poppa Fox asked, casting a sideways glance at some young sparrows in the tavern. "An angry, wounded fisher in the forest is a danger to everyone who lives nearby."

"It's dead," said Junco. "Killed it."

The eavesdropping patrons looked stunned by the claim.

"Remarkable," Poppa Fox murmured, dumbfounded. Then the old innkeeper turned to Cyrus. "Son, we don't have a moment to lose! You and Covey go tell the blokes in the field that there is a dead fisher out in the forest." Poppa turned to Junco. "Where is the carcass?"

"Just to the west of here," said Junco. "Under a mound of pine needles. Follow the north side of the pond and then continue straight ahead."

"Good! Cyrus, tell the fellows to find that fisher and see that it's well hidden! If it's one of Teach's cats, and the crows discover it, it will be trouble for all of us!"

Teach's cats? thought Junco. *What could he mean by that?*

Poppa Fox ordered two other sparrows in the tavern to set a watch for crows. He addressed a young, serious-looking sparrow who was standing near the door. "Henry! Henry Clay! Come over here, will ye?"

The sparrow came forward silently. He was dressed in a dark brown hooded frock that covered his eyes and made him look a bit ridiculous, or so Junco thought.

"Young Henry here will attend to your friend," said Poppa Fox to Junco. "Henry knows the wild plants around here better than anybody. What does the goose eat?"

"Gabriel," said Junco. "His name is Gabriel."

"What does Gabriel eat?"

Before Junco could reply, Henry recited: "Berries, seeds, pond plants, tubers, roots, algae, and nearly any variety of grass. A *Branta* goose spends most of its waking hours eating."

Junco was startled by the young bird's knowledge and had to agree. "That just about sums it up!" Henry was an odd, earnest bird and clearly very intelligent.

Poppa Fox chuckled. "Well, Henry, if those are the facts, then you had better get out there and steer that *Branta* goose away from our fields and toward something in the pond."

"There's some new watercress growing in the pond," said Henry. "Right near the western bank. I'll lead the goose there."

"And, Henry, one other thing," said Poppa Fox. "Ask Gabriel to stay as close to the shore as possible for his safety. I'd like to keep him out of the sight of crows for the time being."

"I'll tend to it straightaway," said Henry without emotion, then turned and flew directly out of the tavern.

"Perhaps I should go with him," said Junco.

"Let's see how he fares," said Poppa Fox, winking. "Go take a look if you like."

Junco went to the doorway facing the pond and watched. As Henry approached Gabriel, the goose reared back. Junco worried that Gabriel might attack, but the sparrow hovered around the big goose for a bit, and soon the two of them moved together toward the shade of the western bank.

Poppa, who had hobbled up to stand beside Junco, said, "He's a good boy, that Henry." He then shook his head wistfully. "Sad story, though."

"Sad?" asked Junco.

"Ah, his very best friend was murdered just this spring," said Poppa. "By Teach's mob. Henry was with him at the time and blames himself for not saving his friend, though the crows nearly kilt him as well."

150

"I'm sorry to hear that," Junco said, shaking her head. "But why are the crows attacking sparrows? I mean you're . . . ah, we're all Thrushians, aren't we?"

Poppa Fox paused and looked skeptically at Junco over the rims of his glasses. "Hmmm, I don't know. Teach seems to be determined to run roughshod over everything these days. Frankly, he's a terror to all of us."

They stood in silence for a moment, then Poppa clapped Junco on the shoulder. "All right, then, enough of that. You must be hungry. What'll you have? My pantry's a bit depleted of seed, but we got some thistle and millet, walnuts. Betcha never had a walnut, have you? And grubs, nice 'n' fresh. Fat midsummer variety. I've got lots of grubs for you."

"Walnuts and thistle will suit me fine, thank you," said Junco. "I'll save the grubs for later, if you please!"

Poppa Fox led her toward a table and soon returned with a basket full of walnuts and thistle and two tankards of mead. While Junco ate, Poppa told her how his great-grandfather had built the Sooty Fox by enlisting the help of fifty sparrows and twenty woodpeckers over the course of three years. "I've lived in this village me entire life except for when I went off to fight for the Thrushians in the war."

The war of which Poppa Fox spoke was the Colonial War between Thrushia and Finchland, a bloody conflict that pitted the serfs of both countries against one another for three long years. Thrushians and finches represented the ruling class in the two colonies, and the serfs were any bird who was not either a finch or a thrush. Swallows, chickadees, wrens, warblers, starlings, and sparrows were the soldiers on both sides.

"I lost me leg to another sparrow who was fighting on the opposite side, for Finchland," said Poppa Fox. "He was a fox sparrow like me, and I swear we looked so much alike that I thought I was lookin' at meself. The two of us stared at each other, suspended in midair with our switches at the ready, and then, I kid you not, we swung our blades and cut each other's leg clean off."

Junco was dumbfounded. "What happened then?"

"The rest of the war is what happened!" said Poppa Fox. "A swarming mess of birds and blades. I never saw that sparrow again."

Junco was eager to hear more, but they were interrupted by the arrival of a throng of villagers, including Covey and Cyrus.

"What's going on, boys?" Poppa Fox asked, scanning their faces. Getting no answer, he turned to an older sparrow, a grizzled-looking farmer. "Joseph? What's happening?"

The old sparrow removed his wide-brimmed hat and stepped forward. "Poppa, may we speak to you for a moment . . . in private?" he said, glancing warily at Junco.

Junco thought that perhaps this was a good time to take her leave. "I'll go check on Gabriel," she offered.

"I think it's best that you stay where you are for the moment," Joseph said abruptly.

Junco did not like his tone and puffed out her feathers.

"Don't mind Joseph. He's a bit gruff. . . . It's his way." Poppa Fox sighed. "Please stay. I'll be back in a moment."

Junco nodded, and Poppa Fox hopped over to join the others, who immediately began speaking in hushed tones and giving sidelong glances in her direction. Junco's heart raced. Had they somehow figured out that she was one of Blue Jay's pirates? She knew that Briarloch was under colonial rule but didn't know where the sparrows' allegiance might actually lie. Piracy was a high crime throughout the colonies, and harboring such a criminal was a felony punishable by death. Turning a pirate over to the authorities would also bring a handsome reward . . . a reward that the poor little village of Briarloch could surely use. Junco was beginning to look for a possible escape route when Poppa Fox returned to the table with a grave expression.

The innkeeper sat down, looking Junco directly in the eye. "These boys were searching for your fisher when they ran into a few wood thrushes who talked of a ship that went down in the forest last night a few miles from here. Which suggests to us that you might be one of the crew from that ship. Might that be true?"

Junco tensed at the supposition.

"Don't worry," Poppa Fox whispered. "Yor amongst friends here. But the crew of that wrecked ship are in terrible danger."

"What sort of danger?" asked Junco.

"They went down near Black Point," said Poppa.

"Teach's territory," said Junco.

"Exactly," said Poppa Fox. "The disabled ship was seized by Teach's mob last night, and from what I hear, the sailors on board did not fare well."

Junco grabbed the innkeeper's shoulders. "Tell me what happened!"

The innkeeper's head drooped. "Many died in the wreck. As for the rest, they've been marooned by Teach. He rendered them flightless and threw them to the ground. I'm afraid that if they didn't find shelter, they'd be helpless against predators and may not have survived."

"Marooned! Those are my mates out there!" Junco said anxiously. "I must find them immediately!"

The sparrows in the room fell silent and stared at Junco.

Poppa Fox tucked in his chin, and his eyes widened. "Yor a pirate, then?" he said.

Junco involuntarily touched the handle of her cutlass and scanned the room, anticipating a challenge, and said in a clear voice, "I am the navigator of the *Grosbeak,* and I answer to no one except my captain, Blue Jay!" At this pronouncement, the sparrows gasped. Junco could tell that they were aware of Blue Jay's legendary reputation. *That may have been a mistake,* thought Junco.

"My mates and I mean you no harm," Junco continued hurriedly. "We are all from poor villages such as yours and —"

"Say no more," said Poppa Fox, holding up a wing. His demeanor was urgent but calm. "I have been waiting and hoping for the *Grosbeak*'s return to Oak's Eye."

Junco was flummoxed by this response. "Our return?" she said. "Why?"

"I'll explain that later," said Poppa Fox. "What we need

to concentrate on now is saving yor friends! I'm sending a scouting party out to find them now."

"Then I'm going with them!" insisted Junco.

"Soon enough, my friend," said Poppa. "But I'm afraid that if you head out now, the crows will capture you in a moment, dressed as you are."

Junco looked down at her black vest and white shirt with its billowing sleeves and cuffs. She looked unmistakably like a pirate.

"No, first we'll get you a new set of clothes that blend in a bit better." Here Poppa pointed to his own garb. "Something like I'm wearing. Gray and brown! No one takes notice of us wearing these clothes. We're just LBB."

Junco looked puzzled. "LBB?"

"Little bland birds. We're all but invisible in the forest! And that, my friend, is how we like it!"

II

HILLARY

Hillary, the star-nosed mole, lived a quiet, solitary life belowground and was generally oblivious of the toil and tumult of the world above him. For the most part, he lived a peaceful, contented life and spent his days digging tunnels and foraging for whatever food he might find underground: sweet roots or, even sweeter, the grubs that lived in the dirt that surrounded him. He loved dirt, the way it felt against his sides as he tunneled through it, the way it tasted and smelled. Dirt was home, and his home was a vast network of tunnels that twisted and turned, dipped and climbed, and stretched on for miles.

HILLARY

Hillary also loved water but perhaps a little less than dirt. Fortunately, his extraordinarily large paws were excellent for both digging and swimming. Though severely nearsighted (actually, nearly blind), he was graced with a nose that had twenty-two fingerlike tentacles, adept at finding food underground or underwater. He especially liked having fish for lunch and was in Briarloch's pond by midmorning nearly every day no matter the season. Then early in the afternoon, at the same hour every day, he would crawl back to the pond entrance of his tunnel. If he was lucky and the sun was shining, he would linger there awhile, warm his nose, sniff the air, and listen for news from the sparrows, who were always very talkative at that time of day. Their conversations usually centered around gathering food but would occasionally run to gossip about their little village of Briarloch.

Hillary wasn't nosy. He simply liked to hear their chatter. He always greeted them with a polite "Good afternoon, friends. Lovely day, isn't it?" just to let them know that he

160

was present and not eavesdropping. "Oh, good afternoon, Hillary!" the birds would reply, promptly resuming their conversations and paying no mind to the mole. Eventually, Hillary would wish them "Good day" and head back to his tunnel, never having contributed a word to the discussion but nonetheless feeling content, as if he had been a part of something social.

This afternoon was different. Before he could even say "Good afternoon," the birds greeted him in a state of high excitement. "There he is! Hillary! Yoo-hoo, Hillary!"

This caught the mole off-guard. "Who, me?" he asked.

"You're the only Hillary around here, aren't you, Mr. Hillary?"

"Well, yes . . ."

"What have you heard about the pirates? We're dying to know!"

"What pirates?" asked Hillary, feeling suddenly uncomfortable and queasy.

"Goodness, Hillary! You haven't heard? Just yesterday

Blue Jay and his crew shipwrecked not far from here, at Black Point. Teach set upon them right away and marooned the whole lot of them. Kept Jay's ship, the *Grosbeak,* for himself, he did, and left the pirates to be eaten by weasels and fishers!"

"Threw 'em off the ship is what I heard!" said another sparrow. "After clipping more than a few flight feathers."

Hillary had heard legends of both Blue Jay and Teach. To his mind, they seemed like the sort of dangerous, despicable rogues who existed in adventure tales, not in real life. The stories were fascinating, but Blue Jay and Teach were not individuals you would like to meet in the forest. In fact, he thought that they should probably be avoided at all costs. As a result, Hillary didn't quite know how to respond to the news.

"Oh," he said awkwardly. "Well, isn't that . . . remarkable?"

"Remarkable? It's thrilling!" said a sparrow. "A shipwreck! Black Point! Marooning! And a bunch of

grounded, desperate pirates on the loose, or whatever is left of them after the weasels and fishers have their fill!" The sparrows laughed in unison, but Hillary did not see any humor in the story. As a matter of fact, he thought it was frightful.

"And that's still not all," said another. "Two strangers showed up at Briarloch this very morning — a dark-eye and a goose! Both of them dressed real peculiar, I tell you, like ... hmmm ... pirates? And guess what? They claimed to have killed a fisher. Imagine that — birds killing a fisher!" The sparrows laughed again.

Hillary couldn't understand why these birds were so delighted by all of this. Pirates wandering through the forest was trouble, especially if those pirates were capable of killing a fisher. And whoever heard of a goose pirate? These ideas made his throat tighten. He gulped hard. He wanted to ask questions, but the words would not come out.

Hillary felt exceedingly vulnerable, sitting half in and

half out of the tunnel, so he retreated underground completely without saying good-bye to the birds. Once inside his tunnels, he found to his dismay that he still could not relax. He nibbled on this and that and worried about the pirates throughout the afternoon. He tried to do a bit of digging on the new tunnel he had been working on, but his heart wasn't in it. *I'll take a nap, just to calm my nerves a bit,* he said to himself. *A nap always helps put these sorts of things into perspective.* He curled up and, weary from worry, fell into an uneasy sleep.

The words of the sparrows—"desperate pirates" and "fishers"—kept running through his mind, and his dreams were filled with vague images of monstrous things: fanged weasels and bloodthirsty pirates. There were muffled shrieks and strange mumbly voices all around him in the dark.

He tossed and turned for a bit, then startled awake. "What?"

Instead of fading away with the dream, the mumbly voices were alarmingly more distinct, more real.

"Crayee! I tell you we've been down this way before!" said a voice. "Feel these roots here!"

"There are roots all over these tunnels!" said another voice testily. "They all feel the same!"

"Shhh!" said a tinny voice. "There's s-s-s-something right in front of usss! I can smell it!"

The voices were silent for a very long time and Hillary tried not to move, not even to breathe, though his heart was racing so fast that there were no discernible beats, just a steady roar in his ears.

"Give it a poke," whispered the first. "It's probably a dead mole, seeing as we're in a mole's tunnel!"

At this, Hillary became fully awake and animated. His little tunnel was filled with the nasty smell of dirty birds. *Good Lord,* he thought. *It's those pirates!* And then he heard the sound of steel on steel clanging in the dark. Desperate, smelly, dirty pirates with knives! Hillary squealed, flipped himself around, and took off in the opposite direction. He flew through the labyrinth of tunnels like a furry black

165

cannonball, his powerful forearms propelling his body forward with great speed.

How can this be happening? Pirates, here in my home! He headed back toward the pond where he had been earlier that morning. He shot out of the entrance and dove headlong into the water with such force that every sparrow nearby screamed and scattered.

Hillary swam to the bottom of the pond and hid among undulating weeds. There he stayed, holding his breath, and listened. The underwater sounds he heard were muted and eerie, not familiar. Hillary sensed something dark and foreboding in the water behind him. *What's happened? Where are all the fish?* It was then he remembered what the sparrows had said. *A goose! A pirate goose! It must be in the lake!* Panicked, Hillary swam frantically for shore. His head broke the surface, he gulped in air, and his ears cleared to a noisy tangle of sparrow voices shouting, "Swim, Hillary, swim! Swim for shore!"

With sparrows flying and dipping overhead, Hillary swam for his life, all the while bracing for the inevitable pain of being snapped up in the sharp beak of a horrible giant goose pirate who was now out of the water and in the air directly above him!

Just then, a clear, strong voice called, "Gabriel, hold!" Almost immediately the pressure behind Hillary dissipated. The pirate goose had given up his pursuit. The mole reached the bank and pulled himself up by the claws. He flopped over in the sand, then fainted dead away.

A DARING RESCUE

Junco peered down at the strange creature lying unconscious on the shore before her. "Excuse me, but you say
he's a what? A Hillary?"

"He's a mammal," said Henry Clay. "A mole. A star-
nosed mole, actually." Junco had been at the Sooty Fox trying on a less conspicuous sparrow-drab jacket when she
heard the commotion by the pond and flew off to investigate. She arrived just in time to save Hillary from Gabriel,
who had evidently mistaken the mole for something dangerous, like a fisher or a weasel.

The star-nosed mole was, without a doubt, the strangest
creature Junco and Gabriel had ever seen. Its loaf-shaped

body was covered with shiny black fur. Extending from behind was a long, hairless tail like that of a rat. Its front paws were grotesquely large and hairless, covered in scaly, pinkish-gray skin and sporting a set of impressively long claws. But by far, the strangest feature was its nose, with its little fingers that looked like a delicious nest of pink earthworms.

"A comfrey of winterberry should revive him," said a sparrow. "Very soothing, that."

"No, no. He doesn't need soothing," said another. "Throw some water on him. That will wake him."

Henry said, "No, no! You'll scare him to death. I think I know just the thing."

Henry flew to the entrance of Hillary's maze of tunnels, an unassuming hole in the ground partially hidden by long grass, and peered warily in. He shuddered involuntarily, and the others looked at him apprehensively. The thought of being underground was nightmarish to birds. Nevertheless, Henry mustered his will and stepped inside

the tunnel, just a little way. Once his eyes adjusted to the dark, he could make out the smooth, curved dirt walls. Out of the walls poked the roots of plants, dangling like pale white bird's feet. He shuddered again, quickly scooped up a clawful of dirt from the tunnel wall, and walked briskly back out into the daylight.

The sparrows peppered him with questions. "What on earth? What's that you have there? Dirt?"

Henry bowed down and held the dirt under the mole's nose. "There you go — a little scent of your home to restore you." The pink tentacles on the mole's nose began to move, waving toward the freshly dug soil. "Ahummmm," Hillary murmured, as if waking from a nap.

"Hillary? Hello, Hillary?" said Henry.

The mole stirred, then opened his eyes to see the blurry forms of first a sparrow, then an unfamiliar bird who smelled strikingly similar to the mumbling critters who had invaded Hillary's tunnel, and then the giant shadowy figure of—the goose! There it was, towering above him. "All is lost!" cried Hillary, and the poor mole began to weep. "What do you want from me?" he sobbed. "Why are you tormenting me? Please leave me in peace. I beg you!"

"Nobody's going to hurt you, Mr. Hillary," said Henry, gesturing to Gabriel. "The goose here mistook you for something like a small swimming fisher."

"Er . . . a what? A fisher?" said Hillary.

"I'm afraid Gabriel gave you quite a start. My apologies!" Junco actually bowed a bit.

"As well, my apologies," said Gabriel, giving the mole an awkward bow.

"This is Junco and this is Gabriel," said Henry, gesturing to both. "They're sailors who have been shipwrecked near Black Point."

The mole squinted again at the blurry figures around him. He composed himself as best he could, cleared his throat, and said in a measured voice, "If you don't mind, w-w-what I need . . . what I need at this m-moment is a bit of clarity. Perhaps someone could explain to me what is going on here? I'd be pleased to hear, for instance, what brings these pirates, ah, sailors, to Briarloch."

"Allow me," said Junco, who proceeded to tell her story, beginning with the doldrums and ending with the *Grosbeak*'s shipwreck near Black Point and the unknown fate of the *Grosbeak*'s crew. Hillary seemed increasingly excited by aspects of the tale and interrupted a couple of times to ask questions.

By the time Junco had finished telling her story, Hillary could barely contain himself. Something had clicked in his mind. "I can't be absolutely certain, but I believe I may know the whereabouts of your comrades!" He then told of having heard the strange sounds — mumbly creatures and clanging steel in his tunnels. "And might one of them be named Crayee? I remember one said, 'Crayee.'"

"*Crayee!* Those are me shipmates!" Junco cried. "They must be found! Hillary, do you think you are well enough to lead me to them?"

The mole was frightened by the thought of meeting up with pirates again but also buoyed by the spirit of the moment and by the fact that (for once) he was actually needed for something. His tunnels were extensive and complex, full of endless twists and turns and dead ends. It would be very difficult for Junco's mates to find their way out on their own. "Certainly, I'll help you find them. The longer your mates spend in the darkness of my tunnels, the more likely they are to become desperate and unpredictable. We should leave now if you're ready."

"Of course!" said Junco, puffing her feathers a bit to mask her anxiety about venturing into the tunnel.

"Of course, I'll go with you!" echoed Gabriel, puffing himself up as well.

"No, my friend," said Junco quietly. "I'd welcome your

help, but you won't fit in the tunnels, as I'm sure you can see. You'll need to stay here. Hopefully I'll be back soon with our shipmates in tow." Junco patted Gabriel's neck. "Did you know," she asked, "that you flew for a moment as you were chasing the mole?"

"I did a little, didn't I?" said Gabriel.

Junco patted Gabriel's side. "Practice your flying, my friend. You need to fly."

Junco stepped with Hillary to the entrance of the tunnel. There, she hesitated a moment, took a deep breath, and stepped bravely into the darkness.

Gabriel held his ear to the tunnel, listening intently until the sounds of Junco and Hillary faded into nothingness. Even then, he would not be moved from the place.

One by one, the sparrows who had gathered on the shore went home or back to work. Only Henry Clay stayed, perched first in a branch above Gabriel, then settling down on the goose's back. "Don't worry, friend," Henry said. "Hillary is a star-nosed mole, a remarkable, adaptable, capable creature . . ." and so on, encouraging and keeping Gabriel company. Both were determined to stay put till Junco and Hillary returned.

TUNNEL OF HORRORS

There was nothing more comforting to Hillary than being underground. It was a warm, cozy, and secure domain — the best possible place for a mole. In contrast, Junco found Hillary's home to be horribly, unspeakably terrifying. It was dark, dank, and full of multi-legged creatures that scurried across her feet and unseen horrors that tickled at her back like clammy, ghostly claws. The darkness of the tunnel was a profound black that seemed to pour into her eyes, seep into her bones, and stain her feathers with the color of nothingness. Her eyes were as vulnerable as ripe berries ready to fall off the vine or, worse, to be plucked by

some horrible, unseen creature. Finally, she put her wings up in front of her face and stumbled along behind Hillary. The beating of her heart in her ears drowned out the soft padding footsteps of the mole. "Hillary!" Junco called in a panic. "Where are you?"

"Shhh! I'm right here," he answered in a whisper, directly in front of her. "Don't worry. I won't lose you." She could feel Hillary moving on.

"Wait!" Junco whispered.

Hillary paused and Junco stumbled into him. "Sorry, sorry, sorry. But listen, I can't see a thing in here. I am completely blind!"

Hillary chuckled. "Doesn't matter, really. There's nothing to see—just darkness in front of us, more darkness behind us, darkness above and beneath us, and dirt all around us."

"That's not comforting," said Junco, shivering.

"You may find the darkness less disconcerting if you

simply keep your eyes closed and relax. This can heighten your other senses. At least, I find it to be so," he said.

Junco thought for a moment, then asked, "You can't see anything either, can you?"

"No," said the mole. "I'm nearly blind. I don't see much, even bright light, so I see absolutely nothing in here."

"Am I to understand, then, that you navigate this place by, what . . . sound?" Junco asked.

"Mostly by touch . . . and by smell," replied the mole, who then gave a very audible, very wet sniff. "Ah! See there, no offense to your friends, but they are easy to track. They smell — well . . . let's just say they don't smell like my tunnels."

"So you think they're still in here somewhere?" asked Junco.

"Quite certain they are, but we still have quite a way to go, I'm afraid."

Hillary started to press forward, then stopped and

sniffed again, causing Junco to bump into him once more. Hillary murmured, "Listen, Junco, I think you ought to know that in addition to your mates, I've detected another even stronger scent in the tunnel."

"What scent?" asked Junco.

"I'm not sure. However, it is a musky odor, not unlike that of fishers . . . or weasels." Hillary paused. "Can you smell it as well?"

All Junco could smell was dirt. "No. No, I can't," she answered.

"If any of those vermin are in my home," Hillary said with a grumble, "I am not going to be pleased. Not one bit! Despicable, thieving pests, they are!"

"Fishers?"

"No, no, fishers are too big! They'd never fit in my tunnels. No, I'd say weasels are more likely." Hillary sniffed again. "More than one, I'm afraid, at least two, maybe more. We'd better get moving. Let's hope we find your mates before the weasels do."

Junco suddenly panicked.

"Hold on, Hillary!" Junco said desperately. "W-we need a plan."

"I thought the plan was to find your shipmates."

"Yes, I know, but our defenses . . . we have none," said Junco. "And I'm as good as useless down here. I can't fight what I can't see."

"Ah, Junco," said the mole, chuckling a bit. "We're not going to fight weasels if I can help it. We couldn't beat those creatures even if we *could* see them. No, I don't fight under any circumstance! I mean, imagine — me a fighter! Ha! My philosophy is to evade and escape as cleverly as possible! That's my talent, and I don't mind saying I'm quite good at it." He chuckled again. "I know these tunnels because they are a part of me. Right now I can tell that your friends are somewhere ahead of us to the north and that the weasels are approaching rapidly from a connecting tunnel just ahead of us." Hillary paused, listened, sniffed the air again. "Yes, we need to move very fast now. Here, do as I say. Take hold of my tail." Hillary placed his tail in Junco's wings. It felt cold and scaly, like a snake, and Junco wanted to drop it in the worst way, but she held on just the same. "Close your eyes and hang on tightly," said Hillary.

"Why? What are we going to do?" asked Junco.

"I'm going to give you a tow. Hang on!"

Hillary then proceeded to take Junco through the tunnels on a ride that she would never forget. The mole started slowly but quickly built up speed using his powerful forearms, propelling the two of them through the tunnel. Soon the mole was moving so fast that Junco was barely able to keep up. A bird's legs are not well suited for running long distances, and Junco was about to give up when Hillary instructed her to tuck her head down and pull her legs up. The mole sped up still more, and Junco found herself flying through the tunnels at a speed she could barely comprehend. She could feel the tunnel narrow and widen as they went. She could perceive junctions to other tunnels by changes in the air. From one tunnel there would be a short blast of pine scent, from another, the hummocky scent of worms, and from another, the pungent stink of musk. These scents served as signposts for Hillary's subterranean highway, and they were as informative to him as anything Junco knew by sight.

The mole finally slowed his pace enough that Junco touched the ground lightly with her feet, ran for a short while, and then came to a stop when Hillary did. Hillary panted in the darkness. Once he had caught his breath, he sniffed the air of the tunnel. "Can you smell them now?" he asked. Junco certainly could. It was a musky stink that offended her beak. As they stood there, it grew even stronger, bearing down on them in the darkness.

"Yes, it's a terrible smell." said Junco.

" 'Tis, yes," said the mole. "It's a bit narrow right here, so I need you to climb over me to pass and to continue down the tunnel in this direction. Just a little further and you will find your friends. Once you reach them, wait for me, but warn them. You must all be prepared to move immediately when I arrive."

"What are you planning?" asked Junco.

"I'm going to block the weasels' passage by collapsing a section of this tunnel," said Hillary. "But both of us must act rather quickly. So, please, if you don't mind . . ." Hillary nudged her in the dark. "Go, now!"

As Junco squeezed past Hillary, echoing up through the depths of darkness came the loud screeches and trills of the weasels.

"You'll find your friends straightaway, I promise," said Hillary. "I'll join you in a bit. Hurry, please!"

Once past Hillary, Junco drew her dagger and her sword. The weasels were very close, both in sound and stink, yet Junco couldn't move a muscle. How could she abandon Hillary?

Hillary was busy clawing rapidly and methodically at the ceiling, dropping considerable clouts of dirt into the

186

passageway. *Fffoooomp!* came one soft thud after another. With each the sound of the weasels faded, and their stench was replaced by the sweet smell of dirt. *Foooomp!*

Another load of dirt fell close to Junco, burying her up to her thighs. "Oh!"

"Pardon me, old girl," said Hillary from over Junco's head. "Listen, you really must go. I have things under control here . . . unless I bury you by accident. Then we'd truly be in a fix." The weasels' angry screams, even muted by the wall of dirt, sent chills down Junco's spine.

"Go, find your mates," urged Hillary. "Warn them to ready themselves." And with that, Hillary returned to his digging.

LOST AND FOUND

Junco sheathed her sword but kept her dagger handy, stepped out from the dirt pile, and set out to find her mates.

Just as Hillary had said, Junco could smell her ship-mates — dirty feathers, damp clothes, and bad breath.

"Ahoy, mates!" Junco called. "It's me, Junco!" No reply. Junco lowered her dagger and walked forward a bit more. "Ahoy . . ."

"Junco?" came a low and desperate voice from the darkness directly in front of her. The ghost of Chuck-

Will's-Widow? Junco willed herself forward and walked straight into her shipmate's very solid chest.

"Chuck!" exclaimed Junco with great relief. "I've found you!"

"I'm glad yer here, mate," said Chuck, "but Lord! I swear I nearly stabbed you, thinking you were one of them weasels. I'll tell you, I'm awfully glad ye called out when ye did."

"Well, I'm glad for both of us, then," said Junco.

"Tell me quick, mate! Wot's behind you?" cried Chuck.

"A friend. A mole who's blocking the passage of the weasels that are heading our way," said Junco. "I think he's held them off for the moment. Where's the captain? We need to move quickly!"

Chuck exhaled in relief, then called down the tunnel. "'Tis Junco herself, mates! Put yer weapons down!" A muted cheer rose, and Junco recognized the voices of her comrades in the dark.

"There now, folla me," said Chuck. "The captain will

be happy to see, er . . . hear from you." Chuck led her past her six invisible mates, each reaching out of the darkness to touch her and greet her.

"Glad yer alive, old friend," came a particularly welcome voice. "I knew you'd be b-b-back."

"Creeper!" Junco reached out to her friend. "I'm glad you are alive!"

"What'sss become of Gabriel?" asked Creeper hesitantly.

"He's fine. We've found a safe place for him. I'll tell you everything once we're out of here."

Junco then passed by Snipe, who said in a low voice, "I don't know how on earth you found us, but if you get us out of here, I'm indebted to you for life, mate."

"Thank you," said Junco, "but we're not quite there yet! Where's the captain?"

"Crayeee!" Jay reached out of the darkness to find Junco's shoulders. "I knew ya was a great navigator, but this! This trumps it all! Junco, you've saved our skins!"

Jay then leaned in close to Junco's ear and whispered, "You do know how to get us out of this hellhole, don't you? I swear we've about gone mad here, mate!"

Junco was about to tell him, when there was a sudden commotion at the other end of the line. "Pardon me! I'm with Junco. Out of my way, please! Excuse me, I say, let me pass!" Junco recognized the voice.

"Let him pass, mates," called Junco. "He's the true navigator of these tunnels."

The pirates flattened themselves against the wall, and they felt the strange furry shape squeeze past them.

"Captain, this is Hillary," said Junco, doing her best to introduce two figures that she could not see. "He's the mole who —"

"Pleased to meet you, Captain," Hillary interrupted. "Sorry to be rude, Junco, but we really must get out of here quickly. I've blocked the tunnel in two areas, but those monsters are digging fast and they're, well, furious. My barriers may not last for long."

The muted snarls could be heard through the wall of dirt as the weasels dug toward them.

"Please, Captain!" said Hillary. "Order your birds to make a chain. Hold on tightly to one another's shoulders, tails, or whatever they can hold on to and follow me."

Jay made the order. Junco grabbed Hillary's tail, and the rest followed behind. The mole attempted to pick up speed, but the chain broke twice as the birds careened through the twists and turns of the tunnel.

It wasn't long before the weasels broke through the blockades and were tearing through the open tunnel behind them. The weasels' growls and screams followed them and jangled the nerves of every pirate, but especially those terrified birds bringing up the rear!

Hillary came to a sudden stop, causing a pileup.

"Don't stop! Move! Move! Move!" screamed the birds at the end of the line.

Hillary spoke hurriedly. "There is a tunnel on your left

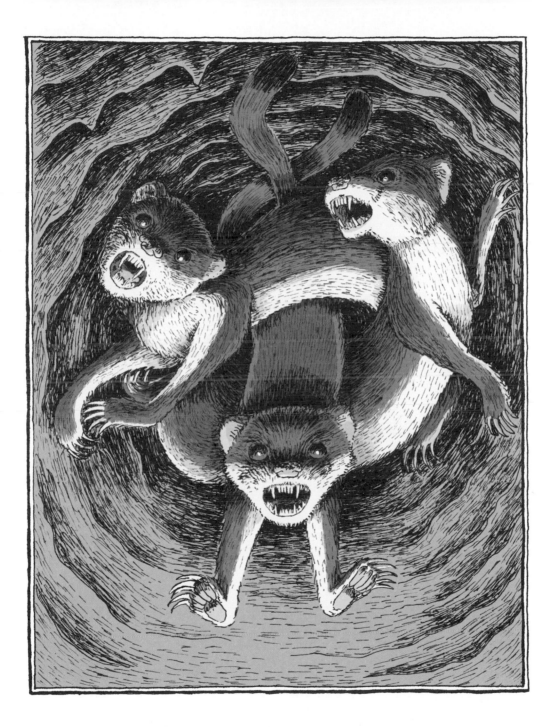

here. Take it! Run as fast as you can. Do not stop for anything. I'll follow behind you. Now, go! Go! Go!"

"Hillary—" Junco began.

"Junco! Go now or, I swear, we will all die right
here!"

The pirates broke to the left then, pouring into the
tunnel, as Hillary stood by to be sure no one missed the
turn. Junco, Blackcap, Jay, Crossbill, Creeper. The weasels
were nearly upon them, now uttering low growls. Snipe,
Thrasher, Chuck, turned the corner.

FHOOMPH! Junco heard the familiar sound of falling dirt mixed with the muffled screams of the weasels. *FHOOMPH! FHOOMPH!* Then there was a sharp
"SQUEAK!" that was followed by a sickening silence.

"Hillary!" Junco cried over her shoulder. She tried to
stop, but the momentum of her mates kept pushing her
forward. They surged through the tunnel and did not
stop until they tumbled, in a filthy pile, onto the shore of
Briarloch's pond at the feet of Gabriel and Henry.

"Captain! Mates!" Gabriel and Henry were shocked by the pirates' appearance. The gosling and young sparrow had waited anxiously, listening for hours, hoping for the return of Junco and the rest of the crew. Given their recent ordeal, the pirates looked more wild and menacing than Gabriel was accustomed to. Henry, who had heard only the legends of Blue Jay and his pirates, was struck dumb in the company of actual pirates. The goose rushed over to Junco, who had taken no notice of him and had begun striding back to the tunnel. "Wait, Junco! Where are you going?" asked Gabriel.

Junco did not answer but stood at the entrance to the tunnel and listened. "Hulloo, Hillary!" she called. No answer. No Hillary. No weasels. No growling, screeching, or squeaking. There was nothing but muffled silence and darkness in the tunnel. "I'm going back!" she declared, then turned and drew her sword and stepped back inside.

"Hold on, Junco!" called Jay. Junco turned to see all seven pirates lined up behind her.

"If you're going back, we're going with you!" said Blue Jay.

Before they took another step, a rustling in the grassy bank startled them. The pirates leaped back and prepared for an ambush by weasels. The grass parted, and over the ridge appeared . . . the mole! His face like a full moon, Hillary smiled down at the pirates. "Good evening, everyone!" he greeted them cheerfully. "Sorry I hadn't the chance to introduce myself earlier. My name is Hillary."

THE PIRATES' TALE

The Sooty Fox was filled to the rafters that evening. Nearly every sparrow in Briarloch was in attendance to gawk in utter amazement at the famous Blue Jay and his crew. The pirates were a sight to behold, all of them dressed in eccentric garb — a motley assortment of colors, shapes, and sizes. Jay regaled the publicans with his tale of the shipwreck, of their encounter with Teach and his mob, and the pirates' last stand at Black Point. "I think you'll all agree, Teach had me in a bit of a bind! I had no weapon, a maimed wing, and the razor-sharp point of a switch pointed at me throat! The tall devil stood there, pickin' his beak with one of my

own feathers and said, 'Aw! Your ship is mine, Jay! Now, tell me, what am I to do with you?'" Jay paused and took a long draw from his tankard.

"What happened then?" asked a wide-eyed Henry Clay.

"Well, now, take a look at this," said Jay, and he held out his left wing to display the blunt remains of his feathers. The sparrows gasped. "Hold 'em up, mates!" And the sparrows gasped as each displayed a wing that was similarly mangled.

Jay continued. "Rather than killing us outright, he decided that it would be more entertaining if he clipped our flight feathers and threw us overboard. And so he did. Tossed us over the rail and down into the hungry jaws of sharp-toothed mammals prowling the forest floor. There we were, marooned in the underbrush at night with grim prospects, unable to fly and with nothing to save us except a few knives and our wits!"

The sparrows stared, wide-eyed and mute, as Jay continued: "The bloodred eyes of weasels burned like coals in the dark that surrounded us; their cruel snarls and screams filled the forest. The devils were so close that we could smell the foulness of their breath! I'm sure we would have been eaten, if it weren't for the resourcefulness of my good crew, especially of this ruffian here," said Jay, nodding to Chuck. "Master Will's-Widow, the first to be tossed off the ship, had the good sense to seek shelter for all his friends, who would shortly be raining down from the sky. He managed to find a hole in the ground that he thought might accommodate all of us, and as we fell, Chuck gathered us in before the weasels had the opportunity to find us. Once we were all safely in the hole, we did our best to fortify the entrance with crude pikes that we fashioned out of long sticks. When those weasels did finally sniff us out, they attacked like an army of demons! We were helpless, or so we thought. Teach had confiscated most of our large weapons, too, so all we had were a few knives and a couple of cutlasses between us. If we didn't think of something quick, we'd all be goners. It was then that Creeper discovered we were not just in a hole but at the beginning of a tunnel. So we blocked up the entrance as best we could and headed blindly into the tunnel, hoping to make our escape." Jay gestured toward Hillary. "Instead we were soon lost in a vast, subterranean maze. We have since come to understand that that maze is Mr. Hillary's home."

"It really is quite cozy," said the good-natured mole to the sparrows. "You should come visit sometime."

The sparrows smiled and tittered nervously at the very suggestion of going underground.

"We weren't seeing anything in that blackness," Jay continued, "just feeling our way along. By the time we stumbled into our host, Hillary, and our friend Junco, the weasels had broken through our barrier and were hot on our trail. We managed to evade the monsters for some time, but, I must say, things got a bit sticky down there more than once.

If Hillary had not been there to courageously lead us out of the dark, I have no doubt that by now we would all have been reduced to a pile of feathers and bones."

Jay raised his glass. "Here's to our subterranean saviors, Chuck, Junco, and Mr. Hillary!" said Jay. "We would not be here without you!"

Every bird in the tavern answered, "Huzzah! Huzzah! Huzzah!" and the attention turned to Hillary.

"Tell us wot you did!" cried Chuck. "Tell us wot happened to the weasels."

"We thought you were a goner!" said Thrasher.

"Did you fight them off with your claws?" asked Blackcap.

Hillary modestly waved off the question, but the crowd would not relent. "Aw, come on. Tell us!"

"Ye didn't eat them, did ye?" called Chuck, and the room erupted into laughter.

"You're asking me to give away my secrets," said Hillary, "but all right! All right! I'll tell you the story, but, you know, there's really not much to tell."

The room quieted, and the soft-spoken mole told his story. "As you may know, I like to dig. I dig just below the surface of the ground to find food, I dig deep down underground to find warmth in the winter or coolness in the summer, and I dig mazes to confuse any creature that might choose to invade my home."

"I'll attest to that!" said Jay. "Cry-ee-aye!"

"Every so often in my digging," Hillary continued, "I inadvertently tunnel into the dens of other mammals."

"What sort of mammals?" asked Henry Clay anxiously.

"Well, let's see . . . ," said Hillary. "Rabbits, mice, chipmunks, badgers, fox, wolves, and occasionally a bear."

"OOOOOOOH!" said the crowd.

"Usually I repair and close up these mistakes, but with the larger animals, I might just leave the opening as a trap or a trick for any unwelcome guests that might trespass into my tunnels. This evening, for example, I managed to successfully facilitate a visit between our unwitting weasels and a she wolf tending to her pups. Wolf mothers with babies don't like to be disturbed. I didn't linger too long to find out how the visit went, but from what I could hear, I think it's safe to say that those particular weasels won't be bothering us again anytime soon."

At this, the pirates and sparrows laughed and cheered and patted Hillary on the back.

"Poppa Fox, another bowl of bumble for this fine mole, if you please!" cried Jay.

The tavern had never been so busy. Poppa Fox was like a dervish, spinning plates of food from one waiter to the next, making sure that every customer, especially the pirates, were well served. On that day, the menu included thistle cake with dried berries, suet and pine-nut tarts, baskets of fresh greens and teaberries. He provided dried fish for Snipe, pickled stag beetles for Chuck, and fresh grubs for everyone. His culinary creations were astonishing given the meager ingredients available to him. For drink, he offered up bumble, a potent concoction made from grass and a variety of berries from the forest. The combination of good food, strong drink, and high spirits kept the festivities lively for quite some time. The sparrows of Briarloch found themselves sitting shoulder to shoulder with pirates, sharing food, trading stories, and finding a common bond in the source of their troubles.

"A toast!" cried Jay as he raised his tankard high in the air with his good wing and paused. "To my cousin Teach!"

The room fell silent and the birds looked bewildered.

Jay continued, "May he grow like an onion, with his head in the ground and his feet in the air!"

The pirates and sparrows laughed, raised their tankards, and let out a raucous cheer. "May he grow like an onion!"

"Those crows will feel th' sting of our swords soon enough!" hollered Chuck.

"We'll tear their feathers out, we will!" said Thrasher.

"Aye, Captain!" shouted Blackcap. "We'll take back the *Grosbeak* yet!"

SEEDS OF DISSENT

The party continued through the night. Then it went on as night turned to day and day into night. Three full days after the pirate reunion in Briarloch, Jay had finally run out of stories, toasts, and drinking buddies. By the fourth day, most of the sparrows had drifted back into their daily routines. By the morning of the fifth day, even the pirates had lost interest in the Sooty Fox and began to help out in the village, partly in gratitude to the sparrows but mostly to allay their boredom. Two weeks passed and the pirates showed no sign of leaving.

Gabriel had become especially restless. Having had a taste of swimming in the pond, he wanted more, but Poppa Fox discouraged him from swimming in the open, fearing that the goose's presence would attract the attention of either the crows or colonials flying overhead. "We don't want the Thrushians to suddenly become interested in Briarloch. We don't want them coming by and asking questions 'n' all!" He also requested that Gabriel remove his hat and pirate garb for the same reason. As a result, Gabriel was irritable, and Junco spent most of her days trying to entertain the goose by reading from scrolls she borrowed from Poppa Fox.

Poppa Fox had an excellent library, filled with volumes on the history of Paxwood, the Colonial War, and avian mythology, which Junco thought Gabriel might find especially interesting. Junco read fascinating accounts of the time before the colonies were established, when birds freely migrated and the gods served as peacemakers in the borderless pre-colonial Era. Regrettably, Gabriel seemed

bored by most of this. He listened politely to Junco's reading but rarely commented and never asked questions of her. Instead, he gazed longingly out on the pond and daydreamed.

One morning, Gabriel interrupted Junco's reading to ask, "Why are we still here? What are we doing here in Briarloch?"

"We're awaiting orders from Blue Jay," said Junco.

"What orders? It doesn't seem to me like he has any plan at all!" said Gabriel.

Junco could neither deny nor confirm that. All Junco could say was, "I'm sure he's hatching a plan." Junco set down the scroll and stared up at the sky.

Poppa Fox was growing his own set of worries: Blue Jay and his crew had accumulated quite a tab at the tavern, but so far had not produced a penny in payment and gave no sign of leaving or of having a plan to move on.

One day when the tavern was quiet, Poppa Fox sat down beside Jay, intending to discuss business with the pirate captain. Hillary, who had come to admire Blue Jay and usually hung on his every word, seemed to be dozing on a bench nearby.

Jay wrapped a wing around the tavern keeper's shoulder. "You, sir," said the pirate, "are the finest cacher I've met, and I've been served by a few, as you might imagine."

"Thank you. It was my pleasure t' serve ye," said Poppa Fox humbly. "Yor, uh, welcome as long as ye please."

Jay considered the remnants of his latest meal in front of him. "I've accumulated quite a bill here, haven't I?"

"Larger than most, larger than most," said Poppa Fox, relieved that Jay had broken the ice and broached the subject himself.

"You know that I have nothing to pay you with, at least until I take my ship back from that scoundrel Teach," ventured Jay.

"I thought as much," said Poppa, disappointed by what he knew to be the truth.

"But I *will* pay you!" said Jay hopefully.

"Oh, sure. Sure, I know. I know ye will. . . ." Poppa's voice trailed off.

There was for a moment an uncomfortable silence during which the two avoided eye contact.

Then Poppa Fox cleared his throat and said, "And how is it yor gonna get yor ship back, then?"

"My ship?" said Jay. "Oh, I've got a strategy for that, a plan that I can't reveal just yet. Stealth and surprise — those are a pirate's allies in such matters, you know." Truth was, Jay was stymied by his situation — no weapons, a disabled crew, and no ship — but still he insisted, "I have a plan, yes, indeed!"

"I thought as much," Poppa Fox said quietly. "Care for another drink, Captain?"

"Certainly. Why not?"

Poppa signaled a waiter. "Some more bumble for the captain, if you please!"

The innkeeper waited for Jay to take a haul of his drink, then leaned in close and said, "Captain, if I may, I have a proposal — a plan of sorts — that might be of interest to you and yor mates. One that may help us to achieve what might be considered our mutual goals."

"Really?" said Jay, sitting up with interest. "Aye, and what might them goals be?"

"Woll, that cousin of yors . . ."

"He's no longer a cousin of mine, that rotten carcass-picker," said Jay.

Poppa Fox looked Jay square in the eye. "Rumor has it," he said confidentially, "that Teach is in the weapons business, that he's got himself a full arsenal of metal blades *and* an exclusive arrangement with the Thrushian army."

"You don't say!" said Jay. "That might explain why the Thrushians have turned a blind eye to the villain's exploits!"

"It might, indeed," said Poppa.

"I've crossed swords with Teach, and he does have a fine blade," said Jay, "but the Thrushians produce their own blades. Why would they bother getting tangled up with, and perhaps beholden to, the likes of Teach?"

"Again, it's rumored that the crows have a superior product in the works," said Poppa Fox. "They're producing metal blades strong enough to slice through anything, including, perhaps, yor sword there."

"Well, I'll be spanked!" said Jay. "Teach must have himself a forge, then!"

"Right you are," said Poppa. "But its location seems to be a mystery!"

According to Poppa Fox, Teach had not only developed the ability to smelt and forge metal, but was producing metals that were harder, sharper, and lighter than anything previously made. Such metal weapons and tools were very rare since the process required the use of fire. According to colonial decree, fire was deemed a destructive power in a world made of wood, capable of turning whole forests and villages into vapor and ash. It was an element that seemed to have a will of its own, randomly selecting a ship, fortress, or home to send up in flames. Therefore, colonial law strictly regulated the use of fire by anyone besides those sanctioned by the government.

The crows ignored these laws, believing that they had a unique relationship with fire—one steeped in their origin story. According to crow legend, fire was a gift given to them by "the Great One." As the story goes, the first crow, named Corvus, was a spectacularly colorful bird with a pretty song who was loved by all. The animals in the forest admired Corvus, not only for her beauty but also for her bravery and confidence. (Some might say the crow was arrogant.) During one particularly long, cold winter, the animals became unhappy, held council, and decided to appeal to the Great One to give them heat. Corvus volunteered to make the long journey to the Great One's palace to make the request. The crow flew for three days and three nights. When she finally arrived at the Great One's palace in the sky, she sang her appeal on behalf of all animals. The Great One was moved by Corvus's beauty and lovely song and offered her a flaming branch to take back to the animals in the forest. The Great One warned Corvus that possessing fire was a great responsibility and that with that responsibility would come sacrifice and pain.

Corvus took the branch and began her three-day journey back to the forest. As she flew, smoke and soot from the fire blackened her colorful feathers. When she arrived at the forest, Corvus opened her beak to sing the story of the gift of the flaming branch, but inhaling the smoke had ruined

her beautiful voice. From that day forward, all crows were sooty black and no crow could sing, only croak and caw. In return for this sacrifice, crows alone were gifted with the ability to possess and use fire. Through the ages, crows found new ways to use fire, cooking up medicines and poisons, and eventually forging metal tools and weapons that were far superior to their wooden counterparts.

The Thrushians spent more than half of their treasury (collected in taxes from their citizens) on weapons made by crows. What the Thrushians desperately wanted, however, was the ability to smelt and forge metal themselves, cutting the crows out of the exchange altogether. The crows had managed to keep their technology a safely guarded secret by moving their foundries often.

"I don't suppose you have any idea where Teach has set up his forge, do you?" Jay asked Poppa.

"No, I don't," said Poppa Fox, "but I'd wager that the Thrushians want to know in the worst way. I wouldn't be surprised if the Thrushian government offered a healthy reward to anyone who can provide information on the forge's whereabouts. We've searched for it ourselves, but—"

"Pardon my interrupting." It was Hillary, who till that moment had been so quiet that Jay and Poppa Fox had forgotten he was in the room. "I couldn't help but hear what you have been discussing."

"Yes, and . . . ?" prompted Jay.

"Well," said Hillary, "I'm fairly certain that I know the current location of the crows' forge."

"How's that?" asked Poppa Fox, thunderstruck.

"I said I'm reasonably certain that I know where the forge is."

"Where?" said Jay and Poppa Fox at the same time.

"Well, actually, I believe it may be underground."

"Cry-ee-aye, Hillary!" said Jay. "Come forth and tell us what you know!"

Jay cleared a space on the table in front of him. "And where is my quartermaster? Mr. Snipe?"

"Ah, well . . . I'm afraid I wouldn't know," said Hillary.

"Of course you wouldn't! Why would you?" said Jay with increasing enthusiasm. "Poppa, could you send someone to fetch me first mate and me quartermaster?"

"Shore, Captain," said Poppa. "I'll have Henry fetch them straightaway!"

"And Junco too!" called Jay. "I need my navigator!"

When the pirates had assembled, Jay addressed the group. "Hillary has some news of great import, don't you, Mr. Hillary!"

"Yes, well, I . . ." the mole began tentatively.

Jay patted him on the back. "Now, go on, tell us what you know, my friend!"

Hillary talked for quite some time while Jay peppered him with questions. When he was finished, Jay turned to Poppa Fox. "With this information, we have been presented with an opportunity to fulfill our mutual goal . . ." Jay paused for a moment, as he hadn't quite figured the next part out. "Freedom from tyranny, beginning with those blasted crows."

Poppa Fox looked a bit puzzled. "Yes, well, if that means getting the crows to relocate, then . . . yes."

"Exactly!" said Blue Jay. "I couldn't have said it better! We'll force Teach from Black Point . . . have ourselves a bit of an adventure, and become stinkin' rich while we're at it!" Jay held out his wing to Poppa Fox. "Whaddaya say? Are we partners?"

Poppa seemed baffled but pleased. "Shore. Why not?" he said, shaking Jay's wing.

Junco, Crossbill, and Snipe looked puzzled about the exact nature of this partnership.

THE CROWS' FORGE

Gents," said Blue Jay, "I appreciate your reluctance to climb back into this hole after our last experience in the tunnel." Jay was attempting to assemble a small party — including Hillary, Chuck, Thrasher, and himself — to venture into Hillary's home and investigate the forge. "But I have assurance from a very reliable source that there's a fine prize at the end of the tunnel."

"Wot sort of 'fine' prize?" asked Thrasher.

"The finest swords, spears, and switches you'll ever lay eyes on," said Jay, "made of metal a hundred times stronger than any other, able to cut through an enemy's sword like you were slicing up a block of suet!"

"Beg pardon, Captain, and no disrespect to you, Mr. Hillary," said Chuck, "but how can he have seen any such forge? Seeing as he is blind and all."

"Hillary," said Jay, "tell them what you told me at the Sooty Fox last night."

"Well, let's see . . . ," Hillary began hesitantly. "It was about a month ago that I was digging a tunnel that I hoped would lead to and connect with the north side of Echo Lake. I knew the direction but kept running into rock—"

"No! No!" said Jay impatiently. "Skip to the part about the forge!"

"Well, yes, then," said Hillary. "As I kept digging hole after hole, trying to find a path clear around the boulders, I finally found a vein of soft earth. I dug away at this spot, thinking I was finally getting somewhere, when I broke through to another underground chamber."

"Wot was it?" asked Chuck.

"Well, at first all I knew was that the chamber was full of hot, smelly air. I could also make out voices, then shouts and curses, and finally a high-pitched, ringing rhythmic hammering. *Ping-ka! Ping-ka! Ping!* The smell and the noise drove me back! I sealed the opening with rock, hoping to escape the fumes, but the odor lingered in my nose for quite some time. It was so strong, I could almost taste it. It tasted like metal."

"But did ye see anything?" asked Chuck.

"I don't see very much, really," said Hillary. "But there were definitely birds down there . . . crows, judging by the croaking and cawing I heard over the din of hammers."

"Who'd ever think a bunch of birds would spend that much time underground," marveled Jay. "A brilliant move, putting the forge underground, don't you think?"

Chuck and Thrasher nodded reluctantly; they were intrigued but still very skeptical.

"Crayee! So what do ye say, lads?" Jay pleaded. "Are you up for a little adventure?"

It was then that Henry ran up to the group, bursting with excitement for an adventure with pirates. "I'm ready to join you if you'll have me, Captain Jay!" he said. The other birds barely recognized him, as he was dressed entirely in black from head to toe. His face and tail were painted black as well, and he carried with him a cloth sack and a pitchfork with four lanterns hanging from its tines.

Chuck and Thrasher could barely suppress their laughter.

Henry was not oblivious to his comical appearance and addressed the pirates directly. "I had to disguise myself. If by chance I am seen by crows," he explained earnestly, "I will not be easily identified as a sparrow in this outfit. If the crows have the slightest inkling that sparrows know the location of the forge, they will surely seek revenge on our village of Briarloch."

This truth impressed Jay and silenced Chuck and Thrasher, who now looked upon Henry with bemused admiration.

"Captain Jay," Henry continued, "I have packed seedcakes for everybody, a good bit of water, a length of rope, and four bug lanterns, one for each bird." He handed each of the pirates a small reed cage containing a single beetle.

"Thank you, Henry." Jay looked dubiously at the lone beetle in the cage.

"Don't worry, they'll light up fine once we're in the tunnel," said Henry. He looked to Chuck and Thrasher. "Are we ready, then?"

The two big pirates, shamed and inspired by this little spitfire of a sparrow, nodded sheepishly and agreed.

"Great!" cried Jay. "Let's be off."

"Hillary, you lead the way. Chuck and Thrasher, you're next. And Henry, you take up the rear."

"Take care not to stick us with that devil's fork ye got there," said Chuck.

"Oh, no, sir!" Henry laughed. "This is to protect my back from anything that might attack us from behind." And Henry slung the handle over his shoulder, tines pointed directly in back of him.

With that, the group marched out of the afternoon sun and into Hillary's dark, gloomy home. As promised, the beetles in the lamps opened their wings and gave off a greenish light that illuminated the tunnel all around them quite well. The walls came to life with the twisting tendrils of roots and the frantic darting of bugs hoping to escape Hillary's voracious, searching nose. The experience was at once terrifying and fascinating to the birds.

The light of the lamps revealed that Hillary was much more than an excavator; he was also a masterful sculptor. Rooms feeding into a complex network of passageways were filled with furniture, pots, and utensils, all formed from clay and dirt. These were not crude objects, but beautifully designed and crafted pieces of art. Long, low cabinets embellished with sculpted leaves and scrolls undulated with the contours of the walls. Tabletops were shaped and etched to resemble a bed of leaves, the surface of a pond, or, in one spectacular example, a patch of grass.

Jay stopped and held up his lantern to inspect Hillary's creations more closely. He was amazed to find one chamber full of fantastic sculptures, one of a beetle and the other of a cricket, both the size of a full-grown bird. Jay whistled softly and shook his head in admiration.

After a time, they reached a rough and crumbly passageway, where Hillary stopped, then whispered, "This is the tunnel that leads to the forge. We must be especially quiet from here on. We are very close." Hillary resumed his lead. "Leave your lamps here and follow me."

The mole and the four birds followed the tunnel as it curved around the smooth stone face of a boulder and led eventually to a dead end. Hillary stopped. "This is the place," he said. "Are you ready?"

"Ready," said Jay.

"Stand by for a moment," said Hillary. The birds waited in the dark, listening to the mole's digging. Then, "Here goes," Hillary said, and they heard the soft thud of a heavy stone falling away. Brown light, along with a blast of hot, putrid air, spilled into the tunnel. The sharp, loud sounds of hammers pounding metal clashed with the curses of the crows screaming at one another over the din.

Hillary beckoned the birds toward the small opening he'd made. They peered through the hole and could not believe their eyes!

Hillary had indeed stumbled upon Teach's forge and armory, a large underground chamber full of crows, molten metal, and extremely valuable weapons. Disorderly workers cursed at one another as they hammered swords on the flat stone floor. Others shaped and sharpened blades using the wall of the cave as a sharpening stone. In another area a group of younger crows attached hilts and elaborately carved handles of black wood to knives, swords, spears, and axes. More than two dozen finished weapons lined the walls, tantalizingly close to Hillary's tunnel, their polished metal blades reflecting the light from the forge, which produced blasts of fire.

Jay was smitten. "Cryee!" he whispered. "If that isn't a sight! I wish you could see this, Hillary, because it's beyond description."

"Oh, I'll be satisfied enough," said the mole, "once I'm holding a crow's sword in my paws." Hillary was becoming more piratclike by the moment.

"Well, my good friend," Jay whispered, "there are plenty of shining beauties sittin' there, lookin' for a home. I believe one of them is yours! All we have to do now is wait for just the right moment to adopt a few of them!"

The four birds and Hillary spent the next few hours crowded and uncomfortable in the sweltering tunnel, nibbling on seedcakes and watching the forge activities in utter fascination. The conditions of the forge were brutal and the crows were so horrible to one another, it was a wonder that they were able to produce anything at all. Their interactions seemed to be a steady stream of arguments, insults, and threats.

"AW! MOVE YER TAIL, YE DUMB WADDLER!"

"SHADDUP, YA BEETLE-HEAD, OR I'LL CRACK YER BEAK IN TWO!"

"JUS' TRY IT AND WE'LL BE POURIN' YE OUT WITH THAT MOLTEN METAL!"

Jay and his cohorts witnessed four fights, one that led to a stabbing from which the victim needed to be carried away.

Yet in the midst of all this conflict, eight crows managed to tend to a caldron that hung over a blazing fire and was filled with glowing-orange molten metal. A short distance away from the fire was a large circular tub made of stones. The tub surrounded a large flat stone on which stood four large crows who were rocking it back and forth while other crows filled the tub with bucket upon bucket of a dark liquid that turned out to be the source of much of the foul smell.

The crows hoisted the molten metal toward a shallow, flat depression in the stone floor. A giant crow with tattered feathers caught the bottom of the caldron with a long hook and slowly pulled back as molten metal poured onto the stone. In the form, the metal took the shape of a broadsword, at first glowing orange, then slowly cooling to a steely gray. The crows grumbled in approval, set down their tools, and fixed their gaze toward an opening above. They remained in this position for a few minutes, waiting. Finally, two burly, clumsy crows flew through the tunnel with a third who was smaller and quite thin. They perched near the forge, looking twitchy and uncomfortable. "Sorry! Sorry! Pardon!" they croaked in turn.

"AW-RIGHT, THEN, YE ROOKS," called the lead crow. "THAT'S A DAY! LET'S GO GET US SOME GRUB!"

Chuck-Will's-Widow recognized the crow. "That's the crumb that splatter-dashed our mates and clipped me wings!" he muttered in a low rumble. "He's gonna have to settle with me sooner rather than later!"

"'Tis him, all right," said Jay. "That there's Bellamy, Teach's less gifted brother!"

"One at a time, y'idiots! Shaddup or you'll attract attention!" Bellamy called, and the crows jostled and fought to be the first out of the cavern. Bellamy strode over to the young crows. "Where've you been?" yelled Bellamy. "Napping, no doubt!"

The crows muttered something unintelligible in response. They were apparently the night shift, assigned to guarding the forge and tending the fires till morning.

"I asked you a question!" said Bellamy. "Where have you been?"

The smallest of the three crows answered. "We had a run-in with them sparras down at Briarloch."

"Briarloch! What were you doing in that mud hole?" asked Bellamy.

"We were flyin' by and thought we'd have ourselves a look-see," said the skinny crow. "They've been acting strange of late."

"Whaddaya mean?" said Bellamy. "They're always strange."

"They've been testy since we . . . visited them last spring," said the other.

Henry heard this and immediately tried to push his way past Chuck and Jay, who clamped his beak shut. "Quiet, Henry!" Jay whispered. "Be patient and you'll have yours, I promise."

The skinny crow continued, "The sparras have become more brazen since then, makin' a tough show of it when we fly by. Tonight they did the same, so we decided to teach them a lesson." And with that he made a chopping gesture with his switch.

Bellamy smiled at this. "Ye didn't!" he said, patting his cohort on the shoulder.

"We did," he replied. "Three of 'em!"

"Well done, then!" said Bellamy. "Get yourselves some rest between watches—you deserve it! Make sure you're up early to prime the forge. I want that fire roaring by sunup, d'ye hear? No excuses!" said Bellamy, and then he took his leave.

With Bellamy gone, the three crows argued over who would take the first watch. Finally they drew straws from which the skinny crow received the short stick. So the skinny crow stood guard at the entrance, while the other two settled down to sleep.

"Time to make our move," Jay said to his four companions. "I'll take the skinny braggart at the entrance. Chuck and Thrasher, you take the other two. Sneak up and knock 'em senseless forever, if you know what I mean." Chuck and Thrasher nodded vehemently.

Henry surged forward. "I'm going, too!" he said, but Jay held him back.

"Not yet, Henry," said Jay kindly. "We're not ready. Be patient, lad!"

"And what am I to do?" asked Hillary.

"Make room in your tunnel, Hillary," Jay said, smiling. "You're about to score a few dozen of the finest crows' swords ever made."

Jay squeezed through the narrow crack and into the forge cave. He then turned to Henry and said, "This may get a bit ugly. Are you certain you want to be doing this?"

"I'm here for Billy!" said Henry. "And I'm here for all of Briarloch. We're tired of being bullied."

"All right, then!" said Blue Jay to Henry. "Stay close by my side."

18

BATS

With some effort, Chuck and Thrasher managed to squeeze through the tight opening and followed after Blue Jay and Henry, creeping quietly along in the shadows of the forge. Without making a sound, each of them grabbed a weapon.

Henry could barely make out the figure of Jay as he approached the sentry. In one swift flash and a silent blow, Jay brought the skinny crow to the ground.

The two remaining crows were dispatched by Chuck and Thrasher.

"Come on, Henry," said Jay, beckoning. "We've got work to do!"

Henry positioned himself just behind the body of the skinny crow, which he and Jay propped up to serve as a decoy. It leaned awkwardly on the shaft of his switch, head listing to one side.

"I need you to watch the entrance, Henry," Jay instructed. "If anyone approaches, caw like a crow to warn us. Can you do that?"

Henry hesitated. "Not really," he confessed.

"All right," said Jay, handing Henry another sword. "Clang these together instead, and we'll take that as our signal to ready ourselves."

"Yes, sir," said Henry earnestly.

Down in the forge, Jay quickly selected the best weapons, then Chuck and Thrasher wrapped each in cloth from Henry's sacks and in the pirates' jackets, including Jay's blue frock, in order to quiet the blades. Each was then passed silently into the tunnel, where they were received by Hillary's strong arms and piled neatly along the walls of the tunnel.

The pirates worked quickly but not near quickly enough for Henry. As the minutes passed and the sky outside darkened, he grew more and more nervous. The natural sounds around him became suspicious and threatening. *Plonk! Pli-plonk!*

"What was that?" From his vantage point, Henry was relieved to see it was only the fish jumping in Echo Lake. But then, out of nowhere came a soft, erratic flap of wings. *Tic-tic-tic-tic-tic-tac-tic!*

Crows! Henry thought, and his heart pounded.

Tic-tac-tac-tic!

But they were not crows. These creatures swooped down sharply, nearly glancing off the water, then veered upward again at the last moment. The air filled with tinny screams. *"Tseee! Tseee! Tseee!"*

Henry started as one of the creatures suddenly landed

at the entrance to the forge, a short distance from where he was hiding. Small and brown, it lurched like a crippled insect between wings that seemed to be hinged in too many places. Its face was both sweet and hideous, with a nose that folded back in on itself, beady black eyes, and large triangular ears. *Bats!* thought Henry. The bat shrieked again, using the sound and its echo to "see," to create an image of its surroundings.

Henry held his breath, but the creature would find him, of that he was certain.

Thinking fast, and in a voice that he hoped sounded crowlike, Henry demanded, "Who goes there? Identify yourself immediately before I cut you to bits."

"Tsee! Tseee!" answered the bat in a thin voice. "You know what I am just as well as I know what you are, little bird. *Tsee! Tsee!* Little . . . sparrow!"

The bat's mocking tone made Henry furious, and he rushed at the bat with both swords clanging, hoping the

noise would shoo him away and also serve as a warning to his mates in the forge. The bat screamed at the sound and flew straight toward Henry.

"Get out, I tell you," roared Henry, "or else!" The bat darted and weaved just out of reach of Henry's swords.

"Who else is in there with you? *Tsee! Tsee!*" teased the bat. "I can hear more breathing and other heartbeats. Little, fast heartbeats, like yours. What are little birds like you doing underground? What are the little birds doing in the crows' forge?"

"Not that it's any of your business!" Henry said, but then tried to come up with an answer to protect the others. "We tend the forge at night; we are slaves to the crows."

"*Tsee! Tsee!* While three of your crow masters sleep s-s-s-s-o silently around you? *Tsee! Tsee!* So silent," said the bat. "This crow sleeps while standing. Curiousss! *Tsee! Tsee!*"

Then Henry heard crows cawing in the distance and, from the sound of it, many crows. He turned his back on the bat and flew into the forge to warn his mates.

"*Tsee! Tsee!* There's no place to run!" screeched the bat after him. "*Tsee! Tsee! Tsee! Tsee!* You are all dead! Dead! Dead! Dead!"

Henry's heart filled with terror and rage, and he clanged his swords together noisily once more to warn his friends. The sound of the crows grew louder as they flew closer.

"*CAW! CAW! CAW!*"

Henry found Jay waiting for him, perched on the rocks above the tunnel. "Stop that racket and get in here!" said Jay. "Quick, Henry," Jay said. "Sweep up your footprints there with your wings! Make haste!"

"*CAW! CAW! CAW!*"

Henry swept away his tracks and hopped into Jay's hiding place behind a pile of rocks just before the crows entered the cave. Behind the rocks were Hillary, Chuck, and Thrasher, who clapped him on the shoulder in approval and whispered, "Well done, Henry!"

"*CAW! CAW! CAW!*"

"Hillary, close the tunnel now!" hissed Jay.

The mole set to his task with amazing speed and strength, rolling the stone back in place and attacking the dirt with his great claws, muffling the angry cries of the crows, who had just discovered that three of their companions were dead and their arsenal had been robbed. Hillary insisted on collapsing a great length of the tunnel to guarantee the crows would not discover his secret home. When he was finished, the pirates retrieved their lanterns and inspected their plunder.

Henry gasped at the spectacular assortment of weapons. There were short, sturdy dirks and daggers, elegant multi-bladed switches decorated with intricate swirling patterns, and cutlasses with blades designed to look like feathers, complete with quills and vanes. Each was beautifully crafted, exceedingly light. These weapons were a far cry from the primitive wooden knives and quarterstaves used by impoverished sparrows.

"Here, Henry, this is yours," said Jay, handing the young sparrow a cutlass. "See what it feels like to wield a quality sword."

Henry stared at the sword with awe and trepidation. The Thrushian government had ruled the possession of steel weapons by sparrows to be a high crime punishable by death.

Nevertheless, Henry shuddered with excitement as he held the sword out and swung it in the air in front of him. The cutlass already felt like a part of his wing — weightless, precise, and powerful.

248

"This one's for Gabriel," said Jay, lifting one end of a giant broadsword, fifteen talons long—half again as long as an adult crow. It was perhaps the most magnificent prize of all. "What do you think, eh, Henry, my young freebooter?"

"I think that our world has just changed," Henry said. "I think that we are also in very serious trouble. That bat knew I was a sparrow, which means the crows now know that I am a sparrow."

"Wot do ye mean?" asked Chuck.

"I mean," said Henry, "I believe that my village is in terrible danger. We must get back to Briarloch immediately!"

19

BLACK POINT

Earlier that evening, Teach entered the dining hall at Black Point, sat down heavily, and stared at the tip of his beak. He was clearly in an ugly mood. Avery ordered more food, thinking that a full gullet might lighten his boss's spirits.

But the heaping bowls that were offered only worsened Teach's mood. "Aw! Naw! Not sparra food! Dratted seeds make me sick! Avery, I swear I'm done with mast. I need meat."

"Aye, sir, I could stand to have some meat myself, but there is none in our stores, not a strip of jerky even. I'll send a scavenger crew out first thing in the morning."

Teach glowered at the pile of seeds in front of him. "You bunch of lazy roosters!" he shouted at his crew. "All ya do is steal from little songbirds!" With a sweep of his wing, he knocked the seeds and nuts off the table and onto the floor. "Not tomarra, Avery! I want my meat now! Tonight, I say!"

"I've got some dried worms here." Bellamy offered his brother a bowl.

Teach pushed the bowl away. "Naw, Bellamy!" he raged. "I want fresh meat! Assemble a hunting crew immediately and find me some!"

Avery looked out at the crew, who looked back at him in stunned disbelief. It was dusk. Soon night would fall and the forest floor would be full of silent, invisible predators with particular appetites for birds. It wasn't wolves or foxes that worried the crows. These were dangerous to be sure, but they were noisy and smelly mammals who were easy to evade. No, it was owls that terrified the crows. Silent, unearthly beings that could snatch a bird right out of the sky, never to be seen again. With muffled wings and razor-sharp talons, they could pierce a victim's skin and carry them away, as silent as a breeze, as invisible as a ghost.

But the crows were saved from just such a dangerous excursion by three bats who came whirling into the hall screaming, *"Tsee! Tsee! Tsee!"*

The crows scattered, turning over tables and drawing swords.

The bats wove past the crows and hovered in front of Teach.

"What is it now?" Teach demanded of the bats.

"We have grave news . . . grave news! *Tsee! Tsee!*"

"Out with it, then!" said Teach, leaning into them.

"The forge has been breached. *Tsee!* Crows have died! Died! *Tsee!*"

The hall filled with the crows' agitated murmurs.

"Silence!" Teach commanded.

The room went quiet, and Teach's eyes narrowed. "Breached by whom?"

"*Tsee,* we cannot say for sure, but there was a sparrow at the entrance. And perhaps more behind."

"*Sparras?*" said Teach incredulously. "Sparras underground? Is this some sort of joke?"

"*Tsee,* we speak the truth. This we know, *tsee.* Three crows at the forge are dead . . . killed. Dead! We have asked our brothers and sisters to watch the entrance to see that no one escapes. *Tsee!* They are trapped. *Tsee! Tsee! Tsee!*"

At the news, Teach flew into a rage. "Awww! Get them, all of you! We will have meat tonight — sparra meat! Everyone! Ah say, everyone to the forge!"

The crows stumbled over one another in a hurry both to get to the forge and to get out of Teach's way.

When the crows arrived at the forge, a storm of black wings filled the cavern. There were no sparrows to be seen, just three dead crows, a depleted armory, and a few bats, who reported that no one had come out of the forge in the time that they had stood guard.

"All right, mates," said Teach. "I want you to search every inch of the cave, but don't touch the floor. I want to take a look at any footprints."

Teach saw plenty of footprints in the dirt, but they were all crow footprints, made earlier that day by the forge workers. Teach flew up to the ceiling to inspect the floor from above. From that vantage point, he noticed something odd. "Look there, Avery!" he called. "Notice the footprints by the north wall?"

"There aren't any footprints there, sir. Swept away, perhaps?"

"Exactly!" said Teach. "Have the boys search the north wall. I suspect we might find a passageway hidden there." The crows found nothing. Hillary had done a superb job of filling the opening. Still, Teach had his biggest crows push at the spot but with no success. "Sparras didn't dig their way in here. Ah think it's a stinkin' mole that did this!"

"Whaddaya mean, a mole?" asked Bellamy.

"Bellamy, you cackle fruit!" Teach railed. "Must I do all the thinking here? Look, there!" he said, pointing to one of the rocks in the north wall. "Notice that all of the stones are clean with the exception of this one?" Teach brushed his wing across the brown dirt clinging to the face of the stone to reveal gray underneath. "This stone was recently moved, then replaced. It still has dirt from the tunnel on it to prove it!"

"You're right, Teach!" Bellamy said, attempting to retrieve his dignity. "Must be a dirty, thievin' mole! Don't worry, brother. We'll dig him out and present his pelt to ya within the hour!" Bellamy turned to the rest of the crows. "DON'T JUST STAND THERE! START DIGGIN'!" he ordered, and a number of crows grabbed tools and began to scrape away at the dirt between the stones.

"Avery, a word!" said Teach, taking his adviser aside. "My brother's an idiot! They're all idiots! But not you, you're clever. Can you tell me something— anything—about moles?"

"Yes, of course," said Avery, matter-of-factly. "They are mammals, they dig extensive tunnels that run for miles, they eat bugs and roots, they're nearly blind and are usually loners."

"Ah, Avery, thank you! We have, at least, a second brain here!" said Teach with a bow. "Now, what do we think are the chances of finding a mole on the other side of that rock?"

"No chance at all," said Avery. "It's moved on. It's far away from here, I'd say."

"Right. And what do our two brains together figure is the likelihood that this mole worked alone here?"

"I would say the mole definitely had help. The bats said as much."

"And who do we think may have conspired with this mole?" asked Teach.

"Perhaps sparrows. That's what the bats told us," said Avery.

"I'll tell you what I think!" Teach scowled. "I think that Blue Jay had somethin' ta do with this. Sparras wouldn't dare steal from us. It's Blue Jay. He's hiding out somewhere around here with my shiny steel. Now, where do you think he's hidin', eh, Avery?"

Avery removed his glasses and cleaned them on his jacket. "The first question should be whom is he hiding with?" said Avery. "Or who's hiding him."

"Sparras!" said Teach.

"Sparrows," said Avery.

Teach ordered the digging stopped and immediately

called for a raid on every sparrow village in the area that very night. He gave his mob permission to "Beat, bleed, or break the bones of as many sparras as it takes to find the whereabouts of Jay and his crew. Don't kill 'em. Just break 'em," said Teach. "I want information first. We'll save the killin' for later."

20

FLIGHT FROM BRIARLOCH

I'd rather die than leave Briarloch to them thieving crows!" said Poppa Fox. "They'll not set foot in me pub or me home. Mark me words, I'll fight them to the death! Me mind's made up. I'm stayin' right here to fight for what's ours!"

Jay and his band of "forgers" had arrived back at the village of Briarloch and warned of a possible full-scale attack by Teach's crows. A hasty plan was devised in which the sparrows would evacuate Briarloch and hide in Hillary's tunnels to wait out the blitz. If the crows invaded, the villagers would be afforded time to organize and launch an attack of their own. Hillary thought this to be a "capital idea." Since Hillary was a stranger to the crows, he would be able to keep the sparrows and pirates safe while giving them time to plan their next move.

Most of the sparrows embraced the idea of hiding but balked at the idea of going underground. However, when faced with the alternative—fleeing into a forest full of owls, weasels, and fishers—hiding in the mole's tunnels for a short time seemed to be the better choice. So, with the pirates' guidance, the villagers headed underground. Not all the sparrows agreed with Jay's plan. There were a few stalwarts conflicted about leaving, most of them veterans of the Colonial War ready to stand and fight in defense of their village. The most notable of these was Poppa Fox. "I did not give up me leg in the war to let crows steal away what is ours! I helped build this village, and I will not abandon it!" he said. "No, I'm stayin' and fightin' for what's ours."

Jay placed a wing over his heart. "We *will* fight the crows!" he vowed. "I promised you two nights ago, and I renew my promise now. We will fight the crows, and we will beat them. With their own weapons, no less! But we can beat them only with a plan."

"Aye, it's yor recklessness that got us into this mess!" said Poppa Fox, feathers puffed.

"It's true. I'm responsible for this mess," said Jay. "But we'll be far worse off if we attempt to defend the village now, with crude weapons and no plan. We'll die as martyrs. It certainly would make for a great yarn for others to tell, but, honestly, I'd rather have them tell a tale of how we defeated the crows, wouldn't you?"

Poppa Fox shifted his weight off his wooden leg. "But this is our home!" he said.

"Please, Poppa, come with us." It was Henry, who had just returned from the tunnel. He walked out of the darkness and up to the innkeeper and took him by the elbow.

"We can't beat them tonight. But we'll have our chance soon enough."

Poppa patted Henry's wing and shook his head sadly. "I am an old bird—"

Just then they were interrupted by the arrival of Junco. "The crows are coming!" she cried. "Our scouts say that they are leaving the forge. If we are going to succeed, we need to get to the tunnels immediately!"

"Poppa?" urged Henry.

"All right, I'll go," grumbled the innkeeper.

Finally, Poppa Fox and all the rest gathered at the entrance of Hillary's tunnel. Gabriel stood guard with Snipe and Chuck. The pirate clothing was gone from the goose, and he looked regal in his natural state. The downy gray and yellow feathers of his brief childhood had turned into sleek black, white, and gray feathers. Gabriel was no longer a clumsy gosling. He stood before them a noble goose.

264

"What's he going to do?" asked Poppa Fox. "That poor fella's head won't fit into the tunnel, let alone the rest of 'im!"

"He and I are going to hide out somewhere at the far side of the pond," said Junco. "We'll keep an eye on things from there until we figure out our next move."

"Won't the crows be suspicious of a gigantic goose floating around in Briarloch Pond?"

"No crow would ever suspect that a goose-god would have anything to do with the likes of Blue Jay and his pirates," said Snipe, "let alone a village of sparrows. Gabriel had fallen overboard before we wrecked, and, besides that, I doubt Teach and his gang would dare attack a *Branta* goose. All he needs to do is keep calm and look uninterested, and the crows will assuredly give him a wide berth."

"And what about Junco?" asked Poppa Fox.

"Junco has gotten good at hiding out with a goose over

the past few weeks," said Henry, with a nod to Junco. "We needn't worry about her. She'll take care of herself. Now, come along, Poppa. We need to get you underground."

Poppa moved toward the tunnel warily, then stopped abruptly and pulled away from Henry. "I'm staying with the goose!" he said.

"Caw! Caw!" The crows were even closer than before.

"But Poppa!" cried Henry.

"Caaaw! Caaaw!"

Hillary poked his head out of the tunnel. "Are you coming or aren't you? I've got to seal up the tunnel now!"

Gabriel reached down and nudged Poppa Fox with his beak. "It's dangerous here," he said. "You need to go. I'm sorry." Poppa Fox wheeled around and tried to push Gabriel away, but the goose grabbed him by the jacket, lifted him gently, and deposited him in the tunnel. Jay and Henry rushed in after him. "Good luck!" Hillary called over his shoulder to Gabriel and Junco, and then the entrance disappeared in a shower of dirt.

"CAW! CAW! CAW!"

Gabriel packed down the dirt in front of the tunnel with his wings. Junco began to help, sweeping the telltale footprints from the shore, but Gabriel urged her to hide. "If the crows catch you here," he said, "we're all goners. I'll finish that. Like Snipe said, the crows won't think to bother with me. I'll be safe."

"Meet me on the other side as soon as you can," said Junco. "I'll be watching out for you."

Just after both birds were out of sight, the crows began arriving. The black forest filled with their croaks, clicks, and caws.

"Spread out! Three of ya to a building! Report back to me!" cawed one crow.

"You heard the boss!" croaked another. "You three, to the tavern. The rest of ya, split up into groups and search the buildings!"

They ransacked the village. Gabriel slipped silently, undetected into the water.

"Aw, they're not here," growled the first crow.

"Check every corner!" said the second.

"They're not here, ah tell ya!" shrieked the first.

"Looks like they left in a hurry," said a third, rational voice. "Don't you think we should —?"

"Aw, someone must have informed them! Spread out! Search the forest!" screamed the crazy one. "I'll not sleep till I've tasted the blood of a sparra! Now, go find me one!"

21

SWIMMING IN CIRCLES

Gabriel shuddered with both fear and indignation as he swam silently in the shadow of the shore. *What is the matter with these birds?* he wondered. *They're all insane. Why would anyone — crow or sparrow — stay in this awful place? For that matter, what am I doing here?* He was alone again, but this time he was not simply feeling lonely. Rather, he felt the overwhelming urge to fly away and never stop, to be anywhere but where he was at that moment.

"What's this, then, eh?" came the raspy voice of a

female crow from somewhere above Gabriel. "A goose? What are you doing here, I'm wonderin'."

Startled, Gabriel began flapping his wings wildly and managed to propel himself a safe distance away from shore but attracted a considerable amount of attention to himself in the process.

"Now you've done it! The others will have heard you," said the crow invisibly over his head. "They'll be on you in a sneeze!"

Sure enough, Gabriel was soon surrounded by an unruly squad of Teach's crows, armed with pointy, razor-sharp switches that slashed menacingly in his direction. "What's going on here, Crookie?" demanded Bellamy.

"Wellll," said the raspy crow, "I seem to have inadvertently startled a sleeping goose. A *Branta,* I believe."

"Aw, Crookie! I don't care what sort of goose it is," yelled Bellamy. "What I want to know is, what's it doing lurking in the pond here?"

Wisely, Gabriel remained silent, his heart beating wildly.

"I told ya, hon," said Crookie. "He was sleeping! Probably resting up before heading south for the winter. That migrating's hard work, I imagine!"

"Crookie!" said Bellamy.

"Ask him yourself, why don't ya?" said Crookie.

"Speak up, goose!" said Bellamy. "State yer purpose!"

Gabriel glared at the crow and hissed.

"Haw! Haw!" Crookie laughed at Bellamy. *"State yer purpose!"* she mocked. "I've no doubt its purpose is being a goose and not having you in his face!"

"All right, Crookie, that's enough out of you," said Bellamy, and addressed Gabriel again. "What happened here, goose? The sparrows of Briarloch seem to have flown off in a hurry! You must have seen something! Speak up, goose!" Bellamy cautiously poked Gabriel's chest with the point of his switch and then flew back. "Speak up or I swear I'll whittle you down to size!" Gabriel was not at all convinced by Bellamy's bluster; in fact, he was more outraged than fearful of the crow.

"Aw, that's uncalled for, Bellamy!" cried Crookie. "If you provoke the poor thing, it ain't never gonna answer your questions!"

"That's enough, Crookie!" snapped Bellamy, and he threatened Gabriel a second time. "Speak up, goose, or I'll start carving."

The point of the crow's switch triggered a powerful emotion in Gabriel. Rage filled his chest and coursed through his wings. From the depths of his soul erupted a sound so forceful and furious that the assembled crows drew back.

"HOOOOOONK! HOOONK! HONK!"

Then a series of powerful wing beats lifted him out of the water and sent Bellamy and two other crows careening backward into the pond with splutters and splashes.

"My, my!" Crookie whistled. "Look at the wings on that boy! Oh! I swear, I'm in love!"

Gabriel felt a new power and confidence, as though something in him had been unlocked by the touch of the crow's blade. He could see more clearly and hear more keenly, and he could intuit what the crows were feeling. They were frightened. They were actually frightened of him!

When Gabriel was through, six crows had been dunked in the pond. The rest remained at a safe distance, including Crookie. "Huh-haw!" she chuckled. "You're quite the character, aren't you, goosey?"

"Aw, it's just an ignorant goose!" Bellamy spluttered as he dragged himself out of the water. "Dumb as mud and useless as a log, I say! It's sparras that we want, anyway. We'll take care of the goose another time. Right now we're off to hunt sparra." On his orders, the crows took to the sky. "Not you, Crookie! You stay and keep an eye on that goose. I don't trust it."

"Yes, sir!" said Crookie dramatically. "I will watch whilst you hunt the mighty sparrow in the forest! Godspeed, Sir Bellamy!"

"Er . . . yes," Bellamy growled. "Yes. And you . . . as well. Don't lose him!"

"Haw! How am I ever going to lose a bird so big? Not to mention one so handsome!"

At that Bellamy simply shook his head and flew into the forest, the rest of his crows following eagerly.

Gabriel began to swim toward a cove that was out of the crow's line of vision and well away from Briarloch, hoping to shake the odd old bird assigned to watch him. But Crookie would not leave him be.

"Where ya goin', handsome?" she teased, flying over his head. "I'm not lettin' you out of my sight, orders or no orders. I'll follow you to the ends of the earth. So, why don't you and I get to know each other? Whaddaya say, mister? Say, you are a mister, ain't ya?"

Gabriel remained silent and aloof.

"Still don't wanna talk, eh?"

Gabriel said nothing.

"Well, if we're gonna be up all night, I don't mind doin' the talking. Keeps me awake, it does. Runs in my family. Insomnia, that is. I remember once, my grandfather told me a story that was a week long. I'm not kidding! I listened to the whole thing and never slept a wink in all that time. It was about this tiny crow named Napoleon, who was about the size of a hummingbird. Well, Napoleon, he developed an attitude on account of his being so di-min-u-tive — that means tiny —" And Crookie was off, launching into what turned out to be a very long story.

Eventually, Gabriel decided to just close his eyes, thinking that perhaps if Crookie saw that he had fallen asleep, she would cease her prattle or, better still, doze off herself. He tucked his head under his wing and waited. Crookie droned on and on.

Gabriel's thoughts drifted. He thought about the oppressed sparrows and about the bullying, demented crows. He wished, more than anything, that he were flying southward. Not that he wanted to abandon his shipmates. No, he wanted them to come with him, but he needed to migrate. Why south, he didn't quite know, but it needed to be south. He had been so restless of late, and an urge to fly had grown overwhelming. Though he had tried several times recently, he had so far succeeded only in planing awkwardly over the surface of the water.

This evening, however, had been different. When provoked by the crows, he had risen out of the water and felt for a moment as if he was actually flying. *I'd fly out of here right now if I knew my friends were safe,* Gabriel thought.

"Snooork!" came a sound from the trees. *"Snoooora-ka-ka-ka-kak!"*

Gabriel opened an eye and peeked out from under his wing.

"Snooork!"

It was Crookie, snoring in her sleep!

Finally! thought Gabriel. Slowly and quietly, so as not to wake the crow, he paddled away.

When he was halfway around the pond, Gabriel stopped to listen. He heard the wind, a few faltering crickets, the deep echo of water lapping up against the bank, the growl of his own stomach, and, in the distance, the crows.

Gabriel hadn't eaten for hours. Plants and minnows brushed against his feet and legs just below the surface, but he did not dare stop until he was back with his friends. He continued paddling along, when he felt something like cold fingers touch his legs. Panicked, he raised his wings and kicked his foot to strike at whatever might be down there. A dark shape swam into view and broke the surface of the water. "Goose," came a sputtering, wheezing whisper. "It's me, Hillary!"

"Hillary?" Hillary's head was barely above the surface of the water, and all Gabriel could see was the mole's nose wiggling in the darkness.

"Shhh! Cover me with your wing!" said the mole.

"What?" whispered Gabriel.

"Cover me," Hillary repeated. "Pretend you are preening so we can talk without being discovered."

Gabriel stretched a wing over his friend and then tucked his head. "Am I ever glad to see you," Gabriel said. "How are the others?"

"They're unhappy but safe. I took them through my

tunnels to an abandoned den on the other side of the pond," said Hillary. "It's crowded and overgrown, but it gives them a view of the pond and Briarloch. I thought that might keep their spirits up."

"Is Junco there?" asked Gabriel.

"She's taken up a position in a tree above our hideout," whispered the mole. "It's a good vantage point, or so she says."

"What should I be doing?" asked Gabriel.

"Be patient. This may take a while. . . ." said Hillary. "As for what to do, Junco suggests you practice your flying skills. Flying might come in handy, very handy soon . . ."

"What is the plan?" asked Gabriel.

Hillary sniffed the air. "I don't know for sure, but I believe Jay intends to make a stand against Teach."

The words filled Gabriel with a surge of excitement in his heart. He knew he was ready to knock a few hundred crows senseless, if it would rid Briarloch of Teach's tyranny and return the pirates to the skies. What was more, he was confident that he could do just that! He wanted to tell Hillary all of this but instead hissed, "I'll be ready!" with such steely determination that it unnerved Hillary.

"Well, so . . . yes . . ." stammered the mole. "I'll come back later with more information. I will pull at your foot, you pretend to preen, and I'll surface up under your wing just as we did tonight. And if you could please refrain from kicking me in the face, I'd very much appreciate it."

"Yes, of course. Sorry about that."

"All right, then, I'm off," said the mole, sniffing the air once more. "By the way, there's a crow watching you from the shore. Take good care and stay calm, goose." And with that, Hillary took a deep breath and dove under, leaving Gabriel alone but with a renewed sense of purpose in anticipation of the battle ahead.

22

CROOKED WISDOM

Good morning, darlin'. Sleep well?" said Crookie.

Dawn was breaking, and in the dim light, Gabriel was barely able to distinguish the crow's silhouette deep within the branches of a nearby tree.

Gabriel remained silent.

"What? Still not talking to poor Crookie?" she said, acting as if she had been jilted.

In response, Gabriel simply turned tail and paddled away.

"What are you doing here, anyway, sweetie?" cooed Crookie in a sincere voice. "You're a goose. You're supposed to be free from . . . all this sort of mess."

Here Crookie caught Gabriel by surprise. He turned around just as she hopped out of the shadows and into the daylight. It was his first look at the crow who had been harassing him all night, and what he saw made him gasp. Crookie was a big old crow, with one dead eye that shone pearly white beneath the short brim of a tattered black bowler hat. Feathers from a variety of birds stuck out at odd angles from the hat's headband. Her large, crooked beak appeared to have been broken many times. She wore a black coat with countless bulging pockets — some with torn seams or frayed edges that revealed bits of their contents: a vine here, a mouse tail there. She bore no weapons that Gabriel could see, but on her back was a rucksack made of skunk fur that looked like a small animal clinging to her shoulders.

Her appearance made him squeamish, and he wanted to redirect his gaze. At the same time, he was determined to look straight into her eyes and not reveal his fear or discomfort.

"Ah! Now you see how horrible old Crookie is. But still,

CROOKIE

you do not fly away," she said in a hushed tone. "You are a polite gander." Crookie hopped out farther on the limb and leaned in close to Gabriel. Her horribly mangled beak barely moved as she whispered, "Fly, goose! Why don't you fly?" She was no longer loud and mocking, but quietly sincere.

Gabriel was surprised by the question. He began to say, "I can't . . ." and then changed to "I won't! I'm staying here till I . . . I've rested, then I'll be moving on!" He immediately wished that he had remained silent.

"Hmmmm. That's better! Now we're talking," said Crookie with a smile. "What's your name, darlin'?"

Oh, why did he speak to her? Now the questions would never end. He knew that he didn't want her to know his real name, so he said the first name that came into his head. "Henry, my name is Henry!"

"Henry?" Crookie smiled as if she knew he was lying. "That's a nice name. Now tell me, Henry, where will you be going once you decide that it's time to go?"

Gabriel had to think quickly, and since he had no idea

285

where he might go if he actually were going anywhere, he said, "North!"

Crookie looked puzzled by this, as fall was coming soon and the cool weather prompted the great southern migration of ducks and geese. Gabriel realized his mistake and said, "South, I'm heading south!" and felt very foolish, indeed.

Crookie did not question his sudden change of direction but looked concerned and asked, "What are you doin' out here alone, Henry? Where's your flock? Have you lost them?"

This put Gabriel on the defensive. He was certain that she was probing to discover the whereabouts of his friends. "Go away! Leave me alone!" said Gabriel, and he swam away from her.

Crookie lit from the branch and hovered over his head, urging him on. "That's it, Henry! Fly! This is a bad place for you. Now, fly! Go to your flock!"

Gabriel flapped his wings and managed to lift himself and his feet out of the water just enough to skim the surface of the pond for a few yards before crashing into the tall grasses near shore.

"That was good! Real good, Henry!" said Crookie from above.

Gabriel had had quite enough of the confounding crow. He snapped his beak at her and yanked out one of her tail feathers.

"*Aaaow!* You monster!" screamed the crow. She retreated to a nearby branch and proceeded to bawl, "Boo-a-hooo! Boo-a-hooo!" The old crow sat hunched on the branch, covered her face with her wings, and wept what appeared to be real tears.

Gabriel moved tentatively in her direction, feeling bad, though no small part of his nature told him to keep his distance.

"Boo-a-hooo! Boo-a-hooo!"

"I'm sorry," Gabriel ventured. "Please — are you all right?"

"Boo-a-hooo! Boo-a-hooo!"

"Please," said Gabriel, moving closer.

"You beast!" Crookie sobbed. "I thought you were something special. But you're just like the rest of us, lashin' out at one another till we hardly resemble birds at all! Boo-a-hooo!"

"I'm . . . please . . . sorry," stammered Gabriel. "I thought you were trying to trick me and . . . and I was angry."

"Angry?" said Crookie, looking up suddenly. Her white eye was now flushed pink. "Let me tell you about the fruits of anger, mister. Better yet, let me show you. Just take a look at me: scarred, bumped and bruised, salty and overripe as a result of holding tight to anger. Now, tell me: what do you have to be angry about? I'm trying to help you, fool!"

Gabriel lowered his head in shame. "Oh. I thought . . . I thought you were teasing me."

"I was trying to talk with you, for grub's sake!" she said, lowering her voice to a hoarse whisper. "I felt sorry for you! You seemed lonely out here. Besides that . . . this is not the best place for you to call home after the drubbing you gave

Bellamy last night. He'll be back to settle up with you once he's slaughtered a few sparrows for his amusement. Have no doubt about that. He's the worst of all of them — greedy, vengeful, and stupid, all in one. So, Henry, as much as I had thought you'd be a decent sort to pal around with, you oughta think about shoving off real soon."

"I won't—" Gabriel began, about to say he wouldn't leave his friends, then thought better of it, still unsure about Crookie and not wanting to give away his alliances. And then he admitted the truth. "I mean, I can't. I can't fly." Gabriel lowered his head. "And my name's not Henry. I made that up. My name is Gabriel."

"Well, that's better, then! You didn't seem like a Henry to me," said Crookie. "Henry the goose. Ha-ha! No, it just doesn't have the proper ring to it, does it?"

Gabriel smiled. "I guess not."

"Now, Gabriel," said Crookie, "what is this you were saying about not being able to fly?"

Gabriel shrugged. "Can't fly yet," he said.

"Oh, sure ya can! I've seen you rise out of the water twice already. All ya need to do is make a couple of adjustments and you'll be cruising. Here, now, give it a try." She gestured toward the water. "Start over near Briarloch and head for the far shore. I'll watch your form."

"All right. All right, I'll give it a try."

Gabriel swam over to Briarloch, which lay silent and still as an abandoned nest. Gabriel shuddered, then turned to face the opposite shore. He took a deep breath, stretched out his neck, and started to churn his legs furiously, as though running. He plowed through the water in a great tumult of foam and spray and splash, pumping his wings up and down, up and down. *Foomph foomph! Foomph foomph!* He felt himself lifting out of the water. His wings rippled the surface with every beat. He was just about to soar higher when the brush on the opposite shore suddenly loomed right there in front of him. Before he could stop himself, Gabriel crashed and tumbled into the brambles, wings flailing, feet snagging on the vines.

Crookie chuckled, which kindled an even fiercer resolve in Gabriel. With a look of determination, he untangled himself from the brush, got back into the water, and turned toward Briarloch for another go. He reared back his head, extended his wings, and . . . he felt something tickling his foot underwater. Without thinking, he kicked it away, then he remembered: *Hillary!* Gabriel aborted his takeoff and pretended to be adjusting and preening his feathers, then tucked his head under his wing and waited for the mole to emerge. Sure enough, Hillary bobbed up from below, sputtering mad.

"*PTTTT! PTTTT!!* What on earth are you doing! *PTTT! PTTT!!* That's twice you've kicked me in the face now!"

"Ooh, I'm sorry, Hillary," said Gabriel. "I'm not used to the feel of your . . . your . . . nose, er, finger things on my leg!"

"Harrumph!" said Hillary, rubbing his nose. "I'm not used to your webbed footlike thing in my face. Anyway,

I'm here to give you a message. We're going to make a stand against the crows at Echo Lake tomorrow morning, and Jay wants to know if you can find your way there overland today. We will be traveling underground and will meet you there. Can you do that?"

"Where is Echo Lake?"

Their talk was interrupted by Crookie. "Did ya break something, Gabriel?"

Hillary dove underwater. Crookie landed on Gabriel's back. "Sorry I laughed back there. It surely was a spectacular landing. Are ya hurt?"

"No, I was just unruffling my feathers before I gave it another try."

"That's the spirit! You almost took off that time, ya know! All ya need to do is start earlier — flap and swim at the same time. Here, eat some of this." The crow reached into a pocket under her wing and produced what looked to be a long, dried rodent's tail and offered it to Gabriel. "Eat up!"

Gabriel drew back in alarm. "No. No, thanks. I only eat plants, thanks!"

"This *is* a plant, silly goose! It's gingin root. It's food. It will give ya the energy to fly, I promise."

Reluctantly, Gabriel took the root, closed his eyes, and took a nibble. He was surprised to find it had a strong but pleasant bittersweet flavor that he found appealing. He ate the rest and felt a warm energy fill him.

"There, that wasn't so bad, was it?" said Crookie. "And here's more for later." She produced another root, attached it to a string, and tied it around Gabriel's neck. "This one's for your long journey home."

The crow launched herself from Gabriel's back and flew a few circles around him. "Now, then, you *will* fly this time. And when ya do, fly as far away from here as ya can until you find your flock. And then, fly with them. Fly south, young goose!" The crow winked at Gabriel. "And then next year, when ya pass through, promise that you'll visit ol' Crookie, won't ya?"

"I promise," said Gabriel. "Thank you, Crookie."

"No thanks necessary. Just promise you'll come see me. Now, let's see ya fly!" said the crow.

Once again Gabriel turned his face toward Briarloch and surged forward. *Foomph! Foomph! Foomph!* His wings drummed the air—three powerful beats and his chest lifted out of the water.

Foomph! Foomph! Foomph! His feet left the water.

Foomph! Foomph! Foomph! His heart surged as he took off to fly over Briarloch. He circled the pond, climbing higher still.

Crookie put on an outrageous show, cheering and diving at Gabriel before she bade him a warm farewell and headed back into the forest.

Gabriel felt a joy unlike any he had felt before. Below him he could see the whole of Briarloch, the *Grosbeak,* Black Point, and what must be Echo Lake—the place where Hillary, Junco, and Blue Jay would be waiting for him.

THE HUNT

They had disappeared! It was as though Blue Jay, his pirates, and the sparrows of Briarloch had vanished into thin air. Teach's mob scoured the forest floor for any sign of the renegades. They searched every den and every nest in every village surrounding Briarloch and interrogated and bullied every bird they met along the way. Word of the crows' rampage must have preceded them, for most of the sparrows had flown into hiding by the time Teach reached their villages. The crows would inevitably find evidence of hasty escapes, half-made meals, abandoned tools and projects. In anger and frustration, the crows plundered what was valuable and destroyed the rest.

Only one settlement the crows visited was still populated by a small flock of what appeared to be a kind of sooty-gray sparrow with brown wings. The crows descended on them, weapons drawn. The frightened birds cowered and pleaded for their lives in a language that none of the crows understood. The sparrows wore plain, drab clothing and straw hats and carried no weapons.

"They're immigrants!" Bellamy whispered to Avery with obvious distaste. "Let's kill 'em all and be done with it."

"Just a moment," said Avery. He strode up to one of the sparrows and held the point of his sword at the poor bird's throat. The rest of the flock began to weep and wail for their companion's life.

"Shut up, ye turds!" yelled Bellamy, but the sparrows only wailed more loudly.

Very slowly, Avery said, "Tell me where Jay is or my crows will quarter each and every one of you!"

"*Ŝpar ni Mi petegi vin!*" the sparrow pleaded softly.

Avery pressed the blade harder. "One last chance: Where. Is. Jay?"

"*Mi petegi vin,*" the bird repeated, eyes wide.

Avery lowered his blade and turned his back on the bird. "Ignorant savages!" he mumbled. Then, "Move out!" he ordered his mob. When the crows hesitated, he yelled, "You heard me! Move out!" and the crows flew off, leaving the sparrows stunned and relieved.

Bellamy swooped up next to Avery. "Why didn't we kill 'em?" he asked.

298

Avery shook his head. "I told that bird we were going to butcher his flock, and he didn't even blink. They didn't understand a word I was saying. Killing them would have been nothing but an enjoyable diversion, one that we can ill afford at this time."

"But they're sparras!" said Bellamy.

"They don't know anything," Avery replied blandly. "Besides, it's getting dark . . . time to report back to Teach."

At Black Point, Bellamy reported having seen no sign of Blue Jay, the sparrows, or the mole.

"They've had thar blasted wings clipped!" growled Teach. "How far could they have gone?"

"We have searched everywhere," said Avery coolly. "There is no sign of them. They have either been saved by a passing ship and are far away or they are still deep underground, perhaps with the mole who broke into the forge."

"If they had hopped a ship, we would have seen them," said Teach. "We would have seen the ship. Naw, they've gone underground, Avery, and that's where they'll die!

Tonight we'll bury them where they lie. I want every hole in the ground flooded or filled with weasels, then sealed and guarded so none can escape."

"Tonight?" said Avery.

"Yeah, tonight. This moment would not be soon enough!"

The gang bristled noticeably at this suggestion. Teach scowled and surveyed the exhausted crows around him. "All right. Tomarra, then!" he said. "We start before daybreak and won't stop till the job is done proper, ya hear?"

"Yes, of course," said Avery and Bellamy.

In the predawn darkness of the following morning, the crows were roused by Bellamy's regular mobbing call. *"CAW! CAW! CAW! AW! AW! CAW!"*

Once the crows had assembled, Teach addressed the mob, outlining his strategy. "We have reason to believe that Blue Jay and his miserable crew have gone underground, as disgusting and unlikely as that might seem. Ah want each of you ta spread out on the ground and search for holes! Ah want every hole found and every hole sabotaged . . ." Teach's word trailed off when a distant but familiar voice drifted through the forest. *"JAY! JAY! JAY!"*

Avery and Bellamy sprang from their perches. "It's him!" they said. "It's him!"

"Yes, it's him, you idiots!" said Teach. "So let's go find him!"

"JAY! JAY! JAY!" came the voice again.

"Get him!" cried Teach. "Get him and get his crew and get them sparras, and this time spare no one! Kill them. Kill them all!"

The crows followed the voice through the forest, past Briarloch, and to the shore of Echo Lake, not far from where they had encountered the immigrant birds the day before. There stood Jay, his crew, and the goose from the pond at Briarloch!

"I knew there was something up with that goose!" growled Bellamy.

301

The crows circled overhead, a large swirling cloud of black against a bright blue sky.

The pirates may have been dirty and bedraggled, but they were armed with pikes from Briarloch and with the weapons taken from the forge. The glint in their eyes and the shine of new steel gave them a fearsome look. All at once, they started up their mobbing calls. The noise grew until it was a cacophony of whistles, croaks, clicks, and shrill screeches: a challenge to the crows, a crazy, poly-phonic battle cry.

In his right wing, Blue Jay held a large, elegantly designed switch. Teach, who had flown up and lit on the branch of a scraggly pine, recognized the switch as being from his own forge.

Gabriel was wielding a long broadsword that had been commissioned by the governor of Thrushia and was created to be displayed in the royal court as a symbol of the colony's power. The blade was four times the length of a normal sword, intricately etched with Thrushian

depictions of heaven and hell: on one side, birds flying toward a sun with the face of a stern owl, and the hilt
sculpted in the shape of a thrush, wings extending toward
the sword point. On the other side, buglike demons drag-
ging faithless birds underground, and the hilt shaped like
a skeleton.

Towering over all other birds, Gabriel was a menacing,
threatening figure. That he possessed this blade, which
the strongest crow among them could barely lift, and was
holding it against them disturbed the crows profoundly.

"You're all holding my property, Jay," called Teach,
"and I intend to take it back."

"This is yours?" said Jay, holding out the switch.
"Really? This looks Thrushian to me." Jay raised the
switch, then plunged it, point down, into the sand.
"This is definitely a Thrushian sword. I thought for sure
you were a corvid, like me. Are you telling me you're
Thrushian, Teach?"

Teach bridled at Jay's insult. "A thrush, ya say?" he yelled. "That is an insult that will not go unanswered!" Teach removed his tall black hat and threw off his long coat. He drew his sword and pointed it at Jay. "I'm neither a thrush nor cousin to you. Why, you're nothin' but a petty thief, a pickpocket, an urchin! Let's say we have it out, once and for all. A duel, ya blue dandy! I challenge ya to a duel!"

"Crayeee!" said Jay, pulling the switch from the sand. "I accept! Clear us some room, boys! Teach and I have a giant score to settle."

THE BATTLE AT ECHO LAKE

In romantic descriptions of sword fighting, duels are a sort of dance involving verbal sparring as much as sword-play. In these tales, the combatants leap from gunwales to rigging to yardarms, crossing swords, trading witticisms, and exchanging barbs with each other. Whether these depictions of sword fights are accurate or not is irrelevant. They are written to create great action sequences. In truth, however, actual sword fights end rather quickly. The duelists face off, exchange formalities, meet in the middle with swords, and hack at each other. He who hacks first often wins.

When it came to hacking, Teach had a certain advantage, being larger, stronger, and taller than Jay. Nevertheless, Avery flew up close to his boss and asked, "Why bother with a duel? Let us kill him and be done with it."

"Yeah," chimed Bellamy. "Finish him off right now."

"I have no intention of dueling. This is a diversion," Teach whispered out the side of his beak. "As soon as I hit the sand, call the attack. Go for the goose first." Then, without warning, Teach left his perch in the trees and plummeted toward the pirate captain, hoping to catch him off-guard. "Good-bye, Jay!" he muttered.

What Blue Jay lacked in size and strength he made up for in wits and agility. He had anticipated just such a deception and was at the ready. As soon as the crow had folded back his wings and dropped into a dive, Jay's reflexes said *Hawk!* and he instinctively rolled into a defensive position for a hawk attack—on his back and holding the switch straight up.

Teach realized his mistake too late and was unable to

pull out of his dive. He screamed as Jay's blade plunged deep into his leg.

As Teach fell, Jay scooted deftly to the side so as not to take the crow's full weight. He let go of the switch and then slashed at Teach with his cutlass, cutting the crow's left wing off just below the elbow.

Teach fell away heavily, cursing, screaming, and holding his mangled wing. "Ya cut me, ya blue devil! Ya cut me!"

Jay moved closer, and Teach took a mighty swing at his head. Jay barely dodged Teach's sword as it came crashing down on his own, splitting it in two and leaving Jay defenseless. Before Teach could strike again, Jay was accidentally broadsided by an errant swing of Gabriel's sword and was thrown clear across the shore.

Blackcap flew to him. "Sir! Are you all right?" he cried.

"Never better! That goose just saved my skin!" said Jay, taking the sword that Blackcap offered him. "Now, let's get back to it!" But when he stood up, he had lost sight of Teach.

By then a full-scale battle had erupted. The crows descended on the flightless pirates. Gabriel swung his magnificent long sword clumsily, as if he were clearing a field with a scythe. Even so, more than a few crows fell around him.

Teach's gang were veteran fighters, experienced in battle and bearing the scars to prove it. They were cocky and confident, boasting and cawing loudly as they fought.

They attacked Gabriel from all sides. This enraged Junco, who flew to the defense of her protégé. "To your left!" she warned. "Behind you! Hold your blade at more of an angle. That's it!"

Jay came charging back to where he had left Teach, eager to knock him off, but two hulking crows blocked his path.

"Kill him!" Teach screamed from a hidden place. "Kill Blue Jay!"

The two crows lunged at Jay. "Cripes!" Jay ducked swiftly under the form of Gabriel. Gabriel made short work of the crows this time with the lethal edge of his sword, separating their heads and tails, which toppled on the beach.

"Well done, lad!" called Jay proudly.

But when he saw what he had done, Gabriel groaned in disgust.

Jay looked up at Gabriel. He knew from the expression

on the goose's face that it was time for Gabriel to fly. "Go ahead, Gabriel!" Jay shouted. "Drop your sword and fly!"

Without hesitating, Gabriel plunged his sword deep into the sand, spread his wings, and took to the air, knocking another crow to the ground with the downward force of his wing beat.

Flying over the lake, Gabriel was no longer the clumsy gosling that tripped over his own feet. He was a magnificent inspiration, a sleek bird with feathers of black, white, and gray. With each stroke of his wings, he felt his heart surge up, up, up, with a force stronger than gravity. The urge to fly was so great that he knew it would be a struggle to fly back to the shore, but struggle he would, if only to bring his mates with him on the journey.

He's fledged! Jay cheered to himself, then laughed aloud. Gabriel was now a force to be reckoned with, something as close to a god as you probably get. Jay leaped as high as his mangled wings allowed, then let out a piercing *"Screeeee!*

Screeeee!" He sounded so much like a red-tailed hawk that the birds on the battlefield cowered.

"Screeeee! Screeeee!" Jay called again.

Bellamy was among those fooled by Jay's call. He sheltered his head with his wing and peered through it to the sky for the terrible hawk that never came. When he realized that he had been duped, his blood began to boil. Bellamy could not stand being made the fool, not again. He flew toward Blue Jay in a full rage, sword slicing the air. "Yer dead, Jay!"

Bellamy's and Jay's blades clashed, and the force of Bellamy's blow knocked Jay violently to the ground and sent his sword flying. Jay heard a bone in his wing snap, and he reeled on the beach in pain.

Bellamy's sword came down again but missed Jay, driving deep into the ground beside Jay's head, so close that he could hear the crunch of the blade entering the earth and the ringing of steel as it was drawn back out.

Jay rolled onto his back in time to see Bellamy lift the

sword high over his head. Just then the forest by the shore rustled with a wild gust of hundreds of wings rising from the ground and through the trees.

Bellamy's eyes shot toward the sound.

"Hear that, Bellamy?" said Jay. "That is the sound of your demise!"

A great swarm of sparrows hit Bellamy from behind and nearly knocked the sword out of his grasp. These were the cousins of the sparrows of Briarloch — sparrows from neighboring hamlets and beyond, and the sparrow immigrants from the settlement that the crows had attacked the previous day. They were little brown and gray birds, and nobody saw them coming. They were led by none other than Henry, who proudly carried a crow's steel sword. They had been hiding in the mole's tunnels that led to the shore. Henry and the sparrows filled the tunnels waiting for Jay's signal. They did not cower at the scream of the hawk but rushed forward, pouring out of the tunnels and shouting their battle crics.

The sparrows flew at the crows' bony backs and beat them with nothing more than sticks and other makeshift weapons. Bellamy tried to fight off the birds, but the crow could barely see or keep his wits about him in the mad confusion. He tried to escape by flying over the lake, but the flock followed him like a swarm of angry hornets. Finally, it was Henry who delivered the fatal blow and buried the blade of his sword deep into Bellamy's chest. "That's for Billy!" he cried.

Bellamy hung in the air at the end of Henry's sword for a moment, as if Henry were holding him up as a prize, triumphant.

"Dirty stinkin' sparra!" Bellamy coughed.

Henry drew out his blade, and Bellamy fell from the sky into the icy water below, where he sank dead to the world into the blue darkness.

The fury of the sparrow horde had the remaining crows in complete disarray. "Retreat! Retreat!" cawed a frantic Avery. As one, the crows turned to fly away, leaving their fallen brethren behind, and the unrelenting sparrows drove the crows well past Black Point, deep into the woods. The crows were completely overwhelmed and scattered throughout the forest. As the cawing of the crows faded, the pirates cheered.

Gabriel landed triumphantly on shore, looking fierce and majestic. His mates greeted him with pats and with embraces around his legs.

"Well done, lad!" shouted Henry. "I don't think those crows are coming back anytime soon. At least, not while you're here."

The determined goose did not hear his friend, nor could he comprehend the crew's joy. His only thought was for his captain, and he strode to where Blue Jay lay on the beach.

Junco, Poppa Fox, Blackcap, and Creeper were already at the side of their dazed and disoriented captain, who was lying with his head propped up in Junco's wing.

"We've won, Captain!" Junco cried, in an effort to rally his strength. "The crows have retreated! We won!"

Jay's response was muted and weak. "Well done, mates. We've won this round for certain." Jay struggled to sit up and fell back again. "Damn! Me wing!" he groaned. "Help me up, will ya, mates?"

Junco called to Chuck and Thrasher, and together they helped Blue Jay to his feet and propped him up, wobbling, between them. Blackcap fashioned a temporary splint for Jay's wing from the shaft of a broken metal sword, wrapping it with his neckerchief.

"Crayee!" Jay said, trying to focus. "That Bellamy packs a wallop!" He pulled away from Chuck and Thrasher. "All right now, gents, let me loose. I need to walk this off." Chuck and Thrasher carefully let go of their hold, and Jay staggered over to Gabriel. He patted Gabriel's side soberly and murmured, "Well done, godling."

Jay then began to look about at the ground, preoccupied. "Ah! Look here, will you?" In the sand at his feet was the distinct impression of a crow's footprints and a dark trail of blood leading to the forest.

"Teach!" said Henry. "So he's still alive."

"Evidently," said Jay, "because this is where I left him."

"We'll find him!" said Henry. "He can't have gone far."

"No," Jay said, shaking his head. "We have more important tasks before us." He looked at the sky. A breeze had blown up and was now hissing steadily through the trees, rocking them back and forth. "We must get back to the *Grosbeak*," he said, then turned to Gabriel with a wince. "Gabriel, would you be so kind as to carry your captain back to his ship?"

Gabriel gladly complied. "With honor, Captain."

A LONG NIGHT

The *Grosbeak* was a wreck. The ship's woven hull was torn open on both sides, exposing her ribs and fragments of her remaining cargo. Fortunately, all of the masts were intact, but many of the yardarms and spars had been snapped off and would need to be splinted and lashed together. Some of the lower sails and rigging were hung up in nearby branches, the lines tangled. Fortunately, the sails were not badly torn.

Snipe ordered his birds to focus on repairs to the rigging. "We'll pretty up the rest of her once we get back to

Oak's Eye," he said, "but for now these holes are a bless-
ing to us. We'll use 'em to toss out any extra weight!" So
toss they did, the work made faster with the help of the
sparrows. Knowing they could not return to their beloved
Briarloch, the sparrows decided that they, too, should
migrate. They realized that the crows would be an increasing problem for them. In addition, it was inevitable that
the crows would inform the Thrushians about what had
transpired at the forge and Echo Lake. The colonial army
would then certainly be descending on the forest. They
would not look kindly on the fact that sparrows had aided
a band of pirates. The sparrows agreed to join with the
pirates on their long journey south.

It was painful for all the sparrows to leave their home,
but perhaps most especially for old Poppa Fox. He had
once again threatened to stay behind, but at Jay's behest
Crossbill offered the innkeeper the position of ship's cook.
"We need us a cook, and yer the captain's favorite cacher!"
said Crossbill.

"Me, a cook on a pirates' ship?" said Poppa Fox, flattered by the offer. "Well, I suppose someone needs to feed all these sparrows, eh?" he said, finally agreeing to join the ship.

Many of the younger sparrows were beside themselves with excitement at signing up with pirates. Hillary, too, had been transformed by the events of the last few days. For the first time in his life, he felt needed and useful. And then there was the excitement! He had also grown enamored of the pirates and was surprised to discover that deep down he was an adventurer at heart. He had even developed a certain piratelike swagger and confidence that endeared him to the rest of the crew. Despite the fact that he was nearly blind, the mole had no trouble feeling his way on board and, given his strength and skills in building, he was quite useful in the ship's rehabilitation.

Snipe ordered the sparrows to throw out the heavy equipment in the galley and nearly every box and crate deemed unnecessary, including many of the crew's personal items.

"The more we throw overboard, the less we'll need to kedge later, mates!" said Snipe. "And let's be quick about it! I don't want to spend another night in this godforsaken place."

Despite his wounds, Jay had insisted on being seated on the upper deck to supervise the repairs. He propped himself against the rail, and from there he called out orders to the crew. But as the day progressed, Jay became increasingly tired. He asked Crossbill and Snipe to take over supervising the repairs. The captain dozed off while the pirates sang as they worked:

> *Weave away! Weave away!*
> *Tomorrow we will thieve away!*
> *Weave away! Thieve away, HO!*

BLUE JAY THE PIRATE

Despite their best efforts, the work was too great to be completed in a single day. By late in the afternoon, it became clear that the pirates would have to spend another night in the forest. As the light faded and the cold began to settle in, Crossbill and Snipe decided that they needed to consult with Blue Jay, who was sound asleep on the upper deck. He looked alarmingly frail.

"Excuse us, Captain," said Crossbill.

Jay did not stir.

"Errr, Captain, sir?" said Snipe.

Again, no response.

In a panic, the quartermaster grabbed the captain's good shoulder. "Captain! Wake up!"

Jay startled awake and wrestled a bit with his coat. "Mr. Snipe!" he mumbled stupidly as he woke. "Crayee, it's getting dark! Why aren't we sailing?"

"We've lost the day, sir," said the quartermaster. "The repairs are too much and the crew is spent."

"Cry-ee-aye, too much," said Jay dejectedly.

"Since our stores have been depleted, I'll order the crew to take supper down below," said Snipe. "They'll have to scrape up what they can find and be back on board in an hour, before the sun goes down completely and the mammals begin their hunt."

"Yes, yes, you do that, Snipe. . . ." said Jay distractedly, looking up at the treetops still swaying in the wind. "Crayee, gents, look at them trees dance! I'm afraid we're in for a wild night."

"It'll be a rough one for sure, maybe in more ways than one," said Crossbill. "How shall we prepare the crew, Captain? Captain?" Jay had fallen back to sleep.

"They'll need some sleep after today's events," said Snipe. "What do you think the chances are that Avery and the rest of Teach's mob will come back to attack us tonight?"

"I think there is a strong possibility," said Crossbill.

"Perhaps," said Snipe. "You might be right. But, then again, there's a part of me that thinks they won't bother."

"Why do you say that?" asked Crossbill.

"Avery would expect us to be on guard all night," said Snipe. "He also knows that we have a goose and a bunch of fighting sparrows on our side."

"He'll attack tomorrow while we're kedging," said Crossbill.

"I'm sure of it," said Snipe.

"Nevertheless, we must be on our guard tonight!" said Crossbill.

"As sure as the crew needs rest for tomorrow's ordeal," said Snipe. "Here's what we'll do: we'll split the watches in two, half the crew at arms for half the night while the other half sleeps. But tell those who are to sleep to keep their weapons handy . . . just in case."

"Agreed," said Crossbill.

Just as Crossbill predicted, it was a rough night. In spite of the arrangements, the crew took little or no sleep.

They were all but certain that they were going to be attacked and killed as they slept. The steadily blowing wind caused the trees to crack and groan long into the night. Every sound, every click, every snap might be the sound of a crow preparing to ambush. The night itself seemed to be made of the dark wings of countless crows enveloping the ship.

The experience was an ordeal for Henry, who while standing guard was brought back to the horrible night his friend Billy had been killed. The cold north wind howled, and with it came the first threat of frost. Henry tugged on his collar, ruffled his feathers, and drew his beak down against the night. He imagined Billy by his side, snoring loudly. Then he heard it — the sound of wings. Something was flying toward him in the dark! He would not fail this time! He slashed out blindly with his cutlass, but his blade sliced through air.

"Stand off!" barked a voice through the dark and the wind.

But a wild rage filled Henry's heart as he struck again and again, each of his blows parried deftly by a wooden staff. "Stand off, Henry!" The intruder forced Henry to the deck and pinned him there. Henry continued to struggle for a moment, then looked up to see a familiar face staring down at him. "Billy! Junco!" he said with alarm. "I'm sorry. I thought—"

"It's OK. I know what you thought," said Junco, releasing the young sparrow and helping him to his feet. "It's OK. You're going to be fine. Snipe has canceled the watch and ordered everyone to take shelter! It's too dangerous out here. Come and warm yourself next to Gabriel and Hillary."

Henry hesitated.

"Quartermaster's orders!" prompted Junco.

Henry, Junco, and Hillary huddled under Gabriel's wings. Junco passed Henry a basket of seed. "Here, have some food and try to get some sleep." Henry took some seed, nibbled it numbly, then fell into an exhausted sleep.

The wind continued to howl, sounding like all the voices of the forest speaking at once, including the faint caws of crows and the muffled screams of fishers.

BATTLE FOR THE *GROSBEAK*

The following morning was so cold and bright that it hurt the pirates to open their eyes. During the night a bitter, early frost had swept in that actually froze a number of the crew to their perches, including Creeper and Blackcap.

Chuck came to their rescue by blowing his hot breath on their feet. Chuck's morning breath stank like a corpse on a hot day, and Creeper had to fight off tears as he gagged. "It's . . . ack . . . working! It's working! Oh, Lord!" When the poor birds were finally able to pull their feet from the branches, they flapped clumsily down to the deck, relieved to be free of both the perch and Chuck's breath.

The rest of the *Grosbeak*'s groggy crew emerged, squinting at the brightness of the morning with distaste, and shuffled stiffly into formation on deck. Their feathers were puffed up, and they all wore sour expressions. Clearly, they were not yet ready for the day.

In contrast to his crew, Jay appeared to have recovered quite a bit. The only visible reminder of his beating was that his wing was in a sling. His remarkable transformation cheered the crew. "Junco," Jay ordered, "check the seatings on the masts and see that they are tight to the keel and snug to the deck!"

"Aye, Captain."

"Creeper, scramble up on the yardarms and cut away every other sail tie. I'll be needing those sails in short order!"

"Right away, Captain."

Jay was both excited and uncharacteristically skittish when he asked Snipe and Crossbill, "Do you think the sparrows are ready to kedge?"

"Ready as they'll ever be, I suppose," said Snipe. "I will say that they're excited, which is good, but I don't think they know what they're in for. I suppose that is a good thing for all of us."

"There's not much ship to kedge," said Jay, "so, with or without Gabriel pulling, the sparrows should be able to carry it, don't you think?"

"We need Gabriel!" said Snipe. "I don't want to risk everything on those sparrows!"

You need Gabriel? thought Jay. *Now, there's a shift!*

"But could the sparrows handle it alone?" asked Jay.

"Why do you ask?" said Snipe skeptically.

"Backup plan," said Jay. "One always needs to have a backup plan."

Snipe squinted at Jay. "There's enough of them. . . . I suppose they could carry us to an airstream, though it is not my preferred tack," he said. "We want to be clear of the crows as quickly as possible."

"Of course," said Jay.

"I'm confident that with Gabriel pulling we can make it to the airstream," said Snipe. "I just hope the *Grosbeak*'ll hold together once we're under full sail."

Jay and Snipe both squinted dubiously at their mess of a ship, each wondering how the *Grosbeak* would ever fly.

"I'd like the crew to breakfast before we kedge," said Snipe. "May I —"

"Yes," Jay interrupted, "but tell them to keep their eyes open. There may be crows lying in wait down there in the forest."

Snipe ordered the crew to a quick and careful breakfast "of whatever ye can gather from the ground in an hour." This was a task in itself, as the ground was frozen. Still, they managed to scrape together some food, and by mid-morning they were back on board, preparing to kedge.

"Come on now, mates! The day's a-wastin'!" Jay called, so anxious was he to set sail. "Ye don't want to spend another night in this sinkhole, do you? Get them harnesses on, and quick!"

Jay stayed constantly on alert for any sound or sign of Teach's gang or bats or weasels. He heard nothing. "I don't like it!" he growled to Crossbill.

"Don't like what, sir?" asked Crossbill, as if he didn't already know what nagged at Jay.

"They're out there waiting, aren't they, Bill?" said Jay. "They're waiting for us to kedge."

"Snipe and I believe they are, sir."

Eventually, all the sparrows, Junco, and even Gabriel donned their kedging harnesses. The gander's rig was a complicated mess because of his size. It consisted of a vest and a collar with a loop of rope meant to be gripped in his beak to take the strain off his neck.

Even though the sparrows and Gabriel had proven their worth in battle, kedging a ship was a grueling experience, unlike any other. This would be their first attempt at kedging.

"HEAVE, MATES!" On Snipe's order, the sparrows

flapped and pulled with all their might. "HEAVE US TO THE SKY!"

The pirates stood at the ready, poised to unfurl the sails as soon as the ship cleared the tops of the trees. But the trees resisted giving up their prize and held the hull of the *Grosbeak* in the springy grip of their branches.

"GIVE IT ALL YA GOT! HEAVE!"

While the kedgers played an exhausting game of tug-of-war with the trees, the rest of the crew hacked away at branches until, with much tearing and snapping, the *Grosbeak* finally lifted into the air. The pirates cheered from their positions on the yardarms.

"That's the way, mates!" whooped Blue Jay. "Just a bit higher and soon we'll be sailing pretty!"

The pirates began to roll out the sails as the ship began its slow ascent toward the airstream.

While Teach was an intuitive and impulsive tyrant, Avery was a patient, thoughtful strategist. He had waited and watched throughout the night for the right moment to over-whelm the sparrows and the goose and to kill Jay. He knew Blue Jay's kedging maneuver would provide the perfect opportunity to attack: most of the birds would be defense-less in their harnesses, unable to flee and unable to fight. "It will be like picking berries," he had said to his cronies.

As Crossbill, Snipe, and Jay had predicted, no sooner were they in the air than the crows launched their raid against the *Grosbeak*.

"Here they come, sir!" Crossbill shouted to Jay. "The crows are charging us from below!" Jay looked down to see a sizable mob of crows heading toward them, pursued by a flock of intrepid sparrows, who were doing their best to slow the mob's advance. They relentlessly attacked the crows but could not stop the much larger birds.

Jay winced. The sails were only partially unfurled. "Cryee!! Step it up, mateys!" he called into the rigging. "I'm needing those sails!"

Crossbill and Snipe stood anxiously at Jay's side as the crows drew closer. "Sir?" prompted Crossbill. "Your orders?"

Jay raised his wing and barked, "Mr. Snipe!"

"Yes, sir?"

"It's time for my backup plan!"

"Yes, sir!"

"On my order, cut Gabriel's tether. Do not announce it; do not assign the task to another. I want you to cut the tether yourself, Snipe. Do you understand?"

Snipe looked stunned. "But, sir!"

Jay leaned in close to Snipe. "On my order! Understand?"

"Yes, sir!" said Snipe.

"Crossbill!" called Jay.

"Yes, sir?"

"I need those sails!"

"Yes, sir!"

No more than one hundred feet away, the crows began their battle cries. *"CAW! CAW! CAW!"* Switches and swords were clearly visible in the talons of the angry, bloodthirsty horde.

Jay waited with his cutlass raised. The crows came closer and still he waited . . . waited . . . waited until finally he could see Avery's eyes lock with his. At that precise moment, he dropped his arm and cried, "NOW, Snipe! CUT!"

Snipe cut Gabriel's line, and the gander's sudden release caused the *Grosbeak* to plummet straight down through the flock of attacking crows, scattering them in all directions. It was a brilliant delaying tactic. While the crows were in disarray, Jay screamed orders to the kedging sparrows: "Keep flying! Pull, mates, pull!" The sparrows responded by doubling their efforts. The ship stopped falling and then more gradually began to gain altitude.

The crows, recovered and regrouped, rushed back to attack the defenseless, kedging sparrows.

Gabriel looked to the captain, bewildered and confused.

"HARASS THEM CROWS, GABRIEL!" Jay called to the goose. "KEEP TH' SCOUNDRELS AWAY FROM OUR KEDGERS!"

Gabriel dove into action, flying straight into the mob of crows and knocking more than a few senseless with the sweep of his powerful wings.

"THAT'S IT, GABRIEL!" shouted Jay. "CLEAN THE SKIES OF 'EM!"

Jay looked expectantly up at the mast. The crew on the yardarms seemed to be struggling with fouled lines and the ties that held the sails. Jay hobbled toward Crossbill. "I need those sails, Bill! Order them to cut the ties!"

Crossbill shouted to the riggers, "CUT TIES, MATES! GET THEM SAILS OUT AND CINCHED RIGHT OFF!"

The riggers sliced the tie-offs with their knives, and at last the sails unfurled completely. They billowed and filled with wind, setting the *Grosbeak* sailing once again. The crew cheered as the ship finally rose, heading south.

A few of the kedgers fell in exhaustion and had to be pulled up by their tethers. Still others had been struck down by crows. In the sky just over the masts of the pirate ship, Junco, Gabriel, and the sparrows were still fighting valiantly against Avery's mob. The smaller birds, who had armed themselves with switches and swords, proved effective at throwing the crows off-balance. And Gabriel was magnificent — he showed a force that neither the crows nor anyone else had expected.

342

"Gor!" said Chuck. "Look at that! That goose is not of this world, I tell you!"

Unencumbered by weapons or kedging lines, Gabriel seemed to gain strength with every beat of his wings and every beat of his heart. The wind against his feathers filled him with power and urgency. *"NOW! NOW! NOW!"* he honked, knocking four crows out of the sky with a stroke of his wing. *"NOW! NOW! NOW!"* he honked, sending another cluster of crows reeling.

Avery came spinning up beneath Gabriel in a fury and struck a mighty blow to the goose's side with his switch. There it stuck. Gabriel ceased flapping his wings and hung in the air for a long, agonizing moment. Then, with a tremendous sweep of his wing, Gabriel sent Avery careening to the earth. With effort, Gabriel pulled the switch from his side and lost not a drop of blood. Triumphantly, he threw the switch down and honked, *"NOW!"*

∾∾∾

October 13, 1617, was, by any measure, a very good day for the pirates of the *Grosbeak*. In the end, it was luck and circumstance that won the day. Jay had a feeling that he would cross paths with the crows again, but for now the future seemed full of possibility and excitement, even hope.

"To think it all started with me strange egg." Jay chuckled. "Me egg that would hatch that hissing gosling. The great, stumbling godling; now our swift warrior Gabriel, batting crows from the sky!"

On that cold, sunny afternoon, all animals living in Paxwood Forest witnessed a remarkable sight: a vision so strange and magnificent that it would become the source of myth. Crossing the cloudless blue sky, they saw what appeared to be the wreck of a ship, its wooden ribs exposed and its sides crumbling, yet moving under full sail and manned by a large crew of what appeared to be sparrows!

The ship was flying the colors of a pirate: a black flag bearing a skull and crossbones, better known as the Jolly Robin. And flying in front of the ship, a large *Branta* gander was leading the way like a fantastic figurehead come to life.

Later it was said that on that day, what the animals of Paxwood saw were the ghosts of Blue Jay and his crew being escorted to the afterworld, after having been killed on the shores of Echo Lake in a gruesome battle. Their escort — an enormous goose — was actually a god tasked with delivering the dead pirates to the offices of the afterworld. It was also said that, en route, Jay managed to charm the administrators of the next world into allowing him and his crew to remain on earth under the condition that they help poor and needy migrant birds. Thenceforth, Jay came to be known as the Blue Ghost, the hero of countless tales told to generations of hatchlings.

MIGRATION

In truth, after its crew prevailed over Teach and his mob, the *Grosbeak* limped along the sky toward Oak's Eye Cay, where Jay and company would rest and procure provisions for their long migration south.

The *Grosbeak*'s repair would take some time. It had a hole in its keel that ran half the length of its hull. Its once-smooth weave was now akimbo with sticks poking out in all directions. The broken spars had been lashed together and the sails patched as much as possible. Because the crew had thrown nearly all of the cargo overboard, the ship was "sailing wobbly," creaking and bending with the wind. The masts themselves swayed like saplings in even the hint of a gust.

"Steer us well below the airstream, Junco," instructed Jay, standing on the upper deck with Crossbill, Poppa Fox, and Hillary. "It would easily rip us to bits in our present condition."

"Aye, Captain!" Junco was sublimely happy to be at the helm of her beloved, if crippled ship. No matter, she was under sail once more.

Hillary the mole sat facing west, transfixed by the sun that had begun to set. He sat with his chin on the gunwale and the fingers of his nose wiggling as if trying to touch, to comprehend, the vast array of blurred colors that his weak eyes could barely discern.

"It's going be a dramatic sunset, eh?" said Jay, noticing the mole's interest.

"Aye," said Hillary dreamily. "First one I've ever seen."

"Really?"

Hillary chuckled. "What can I say? I lived underground. But now that I've experienced one sunset, I hope never to miss another!"

"I daresay you are going to enjoy life on board," said Jay. "It's hard to miss a sunset when you're a sailor," he said, gesturing around the ship. Then he, too, chuckled and added, "Unless you are this crew." The lower decks, the railings, and the rigging were covered with sleeping pirates and sparrows in clusters, all oblivious of the specifics of wind, sun, and currents but content in the general pleasure of being on board. Some of the homeless sparrows on board would later settle in the south, while Henry, Covey, Cyrus, and Poppa Fox would remain with the *Grosbeak*, becoming a permanent part of the pirate family.

Jay strode over to Junco. "Let me have a wing at the wheel, mate. I'm eager to feel how she's sailing."

Junco stood aside. "She's sailing a bit better, sir, now that the wind has steadied and the crew's settled."

"Aye, she's all sail now," agreed Jay. "Once we've patched her up, she'll be fine."

The two were silent for a while, the ship creaking a bit as Jay steered the course.

Then Junco blurted out, "Have you had any, um, visions lately . . . sir?"

Jay scratched his chin and said, "Not since that goose out there. At the moment, he is vision enough for me." He continued, "You know, Junco, you were right about that hatchling bringing adventure. Now let's see if maybe he can bring us a bit of treasure, eh?"

"Aye, sir!" said Junco. But she thought, *Adventure, yes, but not treasure. Instead he will bring good fortune. That will be the difference with Gabriel.*

"How about you?" Jay asked. "Have ye had any more of your, ah . . . feelings and whatnot?"

Thankfully, Henry interrupted the conversation, sparing Junco from having to answer. Henry lit on deck, sporting new pirate garb: a black cap, a striped shirt, and a red sash. He also sported such an earnest, determined expression that both Junco and Jay had to stifle a laugh.

HENRY CLAY

Poppa Fox, however, spoke right up. "Lor! Don't you look the part!" he said. "Ye look a proper pirate now!"

Henry, uncomfortable with the attention and eager to begin his first watch at the helm, saluted and announced, "Henry Clay reporting for duty, sir!"

This did cause Jay to laugh aloud. "Crayee, Henry. Ye can take the helm, but I'm ordering you not to salute me again, understand?"

"Yes, sir!"

"Very well, then! Come over here and I'll teach you a bit about steering a ship."

With Jay distracted for a time, Junco took the opportunity to slip away. She was dead tired and wanted sleep. Before she could sleep, however, she wanted to check on Gabriel. Junco flew to the bow of the ship and gazed out at her friend, who filled up so much of the sky in front of her. The goose's transformation amazed her. There was little hint that Gabriel had ever been an awkward gosling, dependent on others for so many months. He had fledged completely into a sleek and powerful gander whose wing-span, as promised, exceeded the length of the *Grosbeak*. It was incredible to believe that she and Gabriel were both birds, let alone shipmates, yet easy to grasp the bond between them.

Gabriel spotted Junco on deck and honked joyfully, proclaiming to the world that these birds were indeed at last heading south. *"NOW! NOW! NOW!"*

Gabriel's call could be heard for miles. To the birds working in the fields below, it was a cry of hope and a call to action.

"NOW! NOW! NOW!"

To the crows in the forest, it was a threat, an audible warning.

"NOW! NOW! NOW!"

To the Thrushians, it was the rumble of a coming storm, the sound of an approaching revolution.

"NOW! NOW! NOW!"

To the pirates and sparrows on the *Grosbeak,* it was simply Gabriel, calling them confidently out of the dark night and into the light of the next day.

"NOW! NOW! NOW!"